The Allagash Tails

MW00817739

THE RANGER'S WIFE

(VOLUME 3 OF A SERIES THAT CHRONICLES THE LIFE AND TIMES OF RANGER JAMES PAUL CLARK)

by
Tim Caverly
and
Franklin Manzo Jr.

Leicester Bay
B O O K S

Newport, Maine

© 2019 by Tim Caverly
Illustrations copyright © by Franklin Manzo, Jr.
Allagash Tails LLC 2018
Millinocket, Maine

Library of Congress Cataloging-in-Publication Data
Caverly, Tim.
Allagash Tails: A Collection of Stories from Maine's "Wild and Scenic River" Vol. 10
Allagash Tails Presents
The Ranger's Wife
The Saga of Jim Clark
Written by Tim Caverly
Compiled by Michael Perry of Leicester Bay Books, Newport Maine.
P.cm.-(wildlife)

Summary: This is the tenth book in the Allagash Tails collection and the third about the life of Ranger James Paul Clark. The story: Susan, the wife of ranger Jim Clark has spent her whole life in the Maine woods. But Mrs. Clark never realized just how resourceful she could be until her husband went to work on the Allagash Wilderness Waterway. Tag along with our lady-of-the woods as she learns early on in life about deadheads only to discover that there are many dangerous things in the Maine woods and every one of them could instantly make her a widow.

ISBN #978-1-7322456-5-5
Printed in the U.S.A.
Second Printing October 2021
Kindle Version also available
About the front cover
Susan King Caverly in Acadia National Park 2019
Photograph from the Tim Caverly Collection

Men are famous for disguising their feelings and shading the truth depending on moods and to whom they are speaking.
However, if you really want to know what a man is thinking, ask the wife. She'll give an honest answer without any camouflage.

--James Paul Clark

ACKNOWLEDGEMENT

We would like to thank aspiring editor Carolanne Young for her help of proofreading a portion of this manuscript. To Matt Perry of the Maine Air National Guard MEDEVAC-Air Transport for *connecting the dots* in explaining the equipment, procedures and methods used whenever our Air rescue crews complete very complex missions to *Preserve Life, Limb and Eyesight*. We extend our gratitude to all of our Armed Services, including Federal, and State personnel who spend their lives protecting others.

We especially want to extend our appreciation to those who wait at home while their Military, Ranger, Warden, Trooper and spouses of first responders stand on the front lines of public safety and search and rescue. And for everything these 'significant others' accomplish behind the scenes that often go unrecognized.

Finally, we wish to thank Michael C. Perry of Leicester Bay Publishing for making the production of this and many of our other works possible.

Sincerely,

Tim Caverly
Franklin Manzo Jr. — August 2019

TABLE OF CONTENTS

DEDICATION

Buzz and Janice Thompson Caverly on their wedding day June 16, 1963.
Photograph from the T. Caverly Collection

This book is dedicated to my sister-in-law, Janice T. Caverly, and to all those who have 'waited at home' while their ranger, warden, trooper, soldier or first responder spouse toiled to protect Maine's natural resources and those who ventured afield.

Speak with anyone who has worked in the natural resource-public safety arena and you will hear tales of dedication to duty, love of community and, as careers progressed, families who moved from assignment to assignment—to locations where they had what some consider sweet and sour experiences. At first feeling despondent due to leaving friends and homes behind; yet gratified for the recognition by superiors, with the feeling of excitement for the new challenges.

A typical work day for these professionals can, in a flash, change from a boring routine to an adrenalin pumping mission to protect life, limb and property. The effort, more often than not, means battling the worst conditions that Mother Nature conjures up only to deliver to a family the heart breaking news of a fatality. While those devoted men and women are 'on patrol' many remain at home–silently worrying, wondering and waiting for their husband or wife to return.

One such person was my sister-in-law Janice T. Caverly. Jan, along with her husband (my older brother Buzz) was well known for her dedication to duty during my brother's 46 years as a ranger and Director of Baxter State Park. In 1963 the 'just married' couple moved to Russell Pond campground where they began 53 years of wedded bliss. Not only was Jan a partner but also a working mother who raised two daughters while fulfilling her own 34 year career as part of the Baxter Park staff.

I first heard about Jan the night Buzz met her at an ice skating party at Cold Stream Pond, in the hamlet of Enfield. He'd returned home smelling of wood smoke from the bonfire, telling me he'd met a girl. The following summer he invited me to join him at his assignment at the Park's distant Russell Pond—a seven mile hike from his car stored at Roaring Brook campground. Early one June morn, before dawn, he shook me awake and announced, "I have today off and we are going to town to get supplies and then drive to Lowell to see Jan."

Rising in the damp predawn and donning back packs, we hiked the first three and one half miles following the weak beam of a two cell flashlight. Once the sun had provided enough light to see the blue blazes that marked the trail, we completed the trek to the Roaring Brook ranger's cabin where we said hi to Ranger Wilber Smith.

After declining a cup of coffee because we were 'off to town,' then seated in my brother's 1956 Chevy, stowed near the ranger's log cabin, we drove to Millinocket to drop off mail, deposit camping income in the State account at the local bank, at last we headed 60 miles to a little settlement south of Lincoln.

Once in the village of Lowell, Buzz would visit with 'friend Jan' while I played with her brothers and cousins. During one such visit on a dark night—in pouring rain—I had my first experience of 'huntin' night crawlers'—four inch long earthworms that had crawled out of the topsoil to escape soggy ground, only to became a fisherman's treasure.

After the visit, we headed north and arrived after midnight back at the Roaring Brook parking lot. There we slept in the car to the tune of country music station "WWWVA Wheeling West Virginia." In a loud voice the DJ would announce "let her go boys" and the airwaves would fill with the country music strains of *"I'm Walking the Floor Over You, Your Cheating Heart, and Give Me That Old Mountain Dew.* Memorizing the words of a favorite, Buzz and I would chime in off-key vocals with *"those that refuse it are few, but I'll shut up my mug if you fill up my jug with sone good old Mountain Dew!"* until we fell asleep—him in the front seat, and me stretched out in the back.

Once the warmth of dawn had broken through the cold dark night, we would slip into our Kelty packs and with brother leading the way, we'd head north and back to Russell, me following as fast as adolescent legs could go. (Past Sandy Stream and Whidden Ponds; where moose standing in knee deep water contently fed on aquatic vegetation.) Onward we trudged slapping deer and horse-flies and feeling pleased when we sighted the gigantic half-way rock, a landmark which confirmed we were only three and a half miles from the ranger's cabin. In the distance, the melodious call of the white-throated sparrow sped us on our way. When suddenly a ruffed grouse flushed chest high across our path, momentarily startled we realized that our sudden presence had frightened a partridge intent on having a breakfast of the red bunchberry. In the crispness of dawn I'd hike with the Christmas tree smell of the balsam fir as the softwood blended with the drifting smell of Buzz's cherry-blend pipe tobacco. Between puffs he'd croon the Buddy Holly classic, "All my love all my kissin'—you don't know what you've been missin'—Oh boy…"

As a teenager I attended their wedding where Jan's brother, Tim Thompson, and I promptly filled the honeymoon couple's suitcase with a box of Uncle Ben's rice. A week later, back at their work-station home, the young couple welcomed me. I spent many summers there exploring and learning the flora and fauna of the Park—thanks to the hospitality of Jan.

When their daughters Cathy and Tammy were born, I continued to be encouraged to visit their summer and, during school breaks, winter homes. Soon Jan became my mentor, encouraging late night conversations about, "How is school? Are your grades ok? How are your mom and dad?" Then listening with a knowing smile when I worried about my latest flame, Beryl Chesley—a perfumed girl with pearly white smile and a knowing look, who could hearten me to hit a back yard baseball home run whenever she asked.

Then there were the countless emergencies. Many a day and night, through the crackle of a two-way radio, I would hear my brother statically question his wife, "There is an emergency situation, can you prepare lunches for the volunteers?" or "Make an arrangement for dispatch of an ambulance?" or "Please call the families of the rescue teams to advise that they won't be home until after an evacuation has been completed?" or sometimes near midnight he'd ask, "Could you prepare a hot meal for some tired members of the search and rescue team?" Jan always complied with all of that and more—with never a complaint.

When Buzz and Jan retired after a combined total of over 80 years of working in the park (not including the countless of volunteer hours they spent off the clock) the couple left many people with personal recollections of good times, secure in the knowledge that the door to the Caverly home was always open. Even though they made tons of friends, I believe that when the twosome drove out of the park for the last time, they left a piece of themselves behind.

On Wednesday August 24th 2016, Janice departed the physical world. That same day, President Barrack Obama created the Katahdin Woods and Waters National Monument; an 86,000 acre addition to the National Park Service generously given to the people of the United States for the enjoyment of and learning about our natural world. When you visit the KWWNM, stand at the overlook, and as you gaze at our spectacular Katahdin—pause for a moment to contemplate, reflect and appreciate the dedication shown by all of those who unselfishly work to ensure today's experiences will last a life time.

Don't be surprised if in the choral song of a white-throated sparrow you hear "Welcome friend—come in and visit for a while."

Blended in the pages to follow, you will find a series of vignettes; while not necessarily scribed in any particular order, they do however recount tales of real life incidents, challenges and adventures. We hope you enjoy your North Woods journey as you paddle along with *The Ranger's Wife*.

PREFACE

Spring in the distant reaches of New England's North Woods is a time of rebirth; sunny days melt frozen precipitation while Mother Nature does her best to disperse the hefty shroud of winter. Throughout the old-growth forest, symphonic sounds are warbled by a feathered chorus—whose refrain is conveyed by a warm summer's breeze. Among the tempos of the White throated sparrows, black-capped chickadees, Canada jays, wood thrush, and rose-breasted grosbeaks, one song stands out above the others.

High over the green softwood needles that carpet the forest floor, a red cardinal perches on the lower limb of a majestic white pine and trills a melody of love to a nearby mate. Focused on the moment at hand, the brilliantly-plumaged male doesn't know nor could he understand the symbolic role of family that he and his spouse represent in Maine's natural world.

Instinctively, the loving male and less colorful, but equally elegant, female understand they are paired for life. Each is comfortable within their relationship. While the feathered husband gathers nest material, the female picks out the location and weaves the accommodations. Before entering their new home, the pair beckons the other with a loud *cheer, cheer, cheer,* or *birdie, birdie, birdie.*

Nor does either understand, or really care that to mankind, the male's bright crimson color with black face mask, signifies wealth, power, and enthusiasm, while the bird's feathered crest represents intelligence. The feathered tuft serves as a heavenly receiver through which some may receive celestial messages, and thus feel the flow of nature. In other words, an open communication through which one may learn their desires, attainable goals, and tranquility—such is the central power portrayed by the cardinal bird.

During winter, the bright red bird flits against a back drop of white exhibiting nature's beauty; a visual calming that reminds us to pause long enough to enjoy the season of blanketed rest. No, the colorful birds don't completely understand what they represent to visiting humans; but they are knowledgeable and comfortable within their own roles.

In today's tale, it isn't by accident that the red cardinal has paused on the limb of a majestic Eastern White Pine—a North Woods giant. This towering evergreen has a life span of 200 to 450 years, recognized by many as one of the most ancient plants on earth—a softwood so respected that the Iroquois felt the white pine was a symbol of peace. The limbs of the conifer, forever green, represent longevity, solitude and fertility, balance, growth, and harmony. Yes, the mighty giant is so well valued that its delicate pine cone and tassel is Maine's state flower. These trees were once so prized that logs with diameters of 24 to 36 inches were labeled "The King's Pine" and reserved by England for use as masts in the Royal Navy.

Today the significance of the red cardinal planning a new family in the arms of the long-living pine, tells a story of reawakening which provides hope and peace to all who pass. It's so comforting that despite the stress of everyday life, humans may find a rebirth of mental and physical health. Thus the Cardinal-with-White Pine becomes a personal symbol of longevity, tranquility and love.

PROLOGUE

In a large vegetable field in Cornville, Maine, a young boy follows his agrarian father through long rows of green beans. Looking sideways, the lad sees crews diligently gathering the ripe crop for harvest. After picking, the produce will be weighed and delivered to the Baxter Canning Company at the company's Hartland factory. The dad has thick black hair which is rarely covered by a frayed ball-cap, wears blue patched dungarees, green t-shirt—stained with sweat—and heavy work boots. A pair of threadbare work gloves dangles from the back right pocket of the farmer's dirty denims.

The six-year-old, costumed to impersonate his favorite television cowboy hero, wears a black western style vest with rearing white stallions embroidered on each side of the front panels. Pinned over his heart on the left panel is a silver colored plastic sheriff's star. Worn under the lawman's vest is a short sleeve red plaid cotton shirt. On a mission only a good guy would attempt, today's young rancher pulls the brim of a black cowboy hat low over his eyes, tightens the adjustable chin strap, and pulls up the black fringed riding chaps that cover his jeans. On his feet, the boy wears a pair of imitation leather western boots.

Striding with confidence, the little cowboy rests his hands comfortably on the simulated pearl-handled grips of the two cap guns that sit easy in pretend rawhide holsters, his trigger fingers extended ready for a quick draw. A wide leather belt secures the toy revolvers on the lad's thin hips. The Roy Rogers look alike keeps a steady gaze at his surroundings in case bad guys attempt an ambush while the boy and his dad survey 'the ranch'.

A young Tim Caverly with his collie dog, Solo
Photograph from the T. Caverly Collection

The father has come for the boy after hearing the boy's orders of "reach for the sky, hombre" to each field hand the lad encounters—a maneuver that distracts the farm's employees from the task of harvesting the family's money crop. With firm instructions the Dad orders, "Stop bothering the workers Jim! Come on now, your mother says it's time for lunch. Today we are having your favorite dessert, fresh strawberry shortcake." Close behind the father and son follows a handsome collie dog, the boy's constant sidekick.

Halfway between the field of vegetables and the farm house the father and son enter a hay field that will feed the family's white-face cattle and their pet horse, Flicka, through the next winter. Walking through the knee deep hay, the tall man stoops to pluck a blade of the waving timothy grass to chew—thankful for any moisture he may gain from the greenery on such a hot summer's day. Mimicking his father, the boy also plucks a long strand and chomps on the bladed stalk. Munching a stem of tall grass during a July stroll through a green field is a habit that every farmer in Cornville, Maine practices during haying season.

One hundred miles to the north, in the town of Millinocket, lives a three-year-old girl with delicate features, hazel green eyes and coal black hair. A baby who laughs easy and will jabber for hours to her mom from a high-chair, only to end the conversation with a baby laugh and a slap of her hand across a tiny knee as if enjoying a private joke.

But today the tot struggles with an illness so severe she has been packed in ice for 24 hours to lower her scorching fever. Doctors, parents and grandparents watch over the family's only child who lies hospitalized in the paper town's small infirmary. They share unspoken worry about the treasured child—Susan. Will she die? Or perhaps worse, will she experience brain damage brought on by the intense malady?

But the girl survives and over time grows healthy enough to spend summers with her river-driver grandfather and a grandmother who works as camp cook for the Great Northern

Paper Company. When not in the woods with Gram and Gramps, her parents take their little girl camping, teaching her about the Maine woods in the wilds of Baxter State Park.

Once she reaches her teens, Susan becomes a councilor-in-training for the local Girl-Scout base where she enjoys swimming, canoeing, and hiking in the park—and where she grows stronger. Often at campgrounds such as Abol, Russell Pond and Katahdin Stream, she sees a young boy who accompanies the local ranger. However, the girl isn't interested in boys; there are too many trails to hike, flowers to smell, and animals to watch.

Nevertheless the girl doesn't go unobserved by the lad. Only three years older, the boy often observes the developing cute black-haired girl with mild curiosity. But he isn't interested in girls and never speaks to her; there are too many brook trout that demand his intimate attention.

A young Susan King Caverly at Girl Scout camp
(the girl, center, in all white staring at the food)
Photograph from the T. Caverly Collection

Seventeen years to the day after the boy is in the field with his dad, and the girl is receiving her ice bath—Jim and Susan meet at college. Two years later, they marry and begin a life in the Maine woods that, in reflection, seems controlled by an invisible force. In the pages to follow, supported by novellas, the reader will discover how a boy from Cornville met a girl from Millinocket while living in a Washington County town; and how such a union endured a relationship that spans over four decades. Their survival as a husband-wife team is a story of discovery, personal loss, hardship, stress, family values, sharing good and bad, while finding friendships never to be forgotten. Theirs is a story shared by many of the men and women who live and work in Maine.

THE RANGER'S WIFE
THE JIM CLARK SAGA
CHAPTER I

Introduction

An investigative reporter contently drifts with the downstream flow of upper Allagash Stream. Meandering with her face raised and eyes slightly closed, the pretty lady basks in the warmth of the morning sun. Her thoughts are interrupted by the splash of a brook trout feeding on caddis flies. Returning her gaze to the river, she uses her paddle like a tiller to keep the canoe parallel with the river's bank—content to move at a snail's pace to fully enjoy the flora and fauna that abounds around her.

After an hour and a half our visitor emerges into a deep water, 4,000 acre inland sea. Leaving the narrow banks of the watercourse behind, she paddles her dark gray canoe across the calm water of Allagash Lake. The mirror-like surface reflects her image of sitting in an Atkinson Traveler; a watery looking-glass sharp enough to reveal the sculptured lines of the homemade craft and that the woman's face is already turning scarlet red from a fresh sunburn. Once beyond influence of the inlet's flow, the paddler rudders the canoe slightly to the north and sculls towards the Ledges Campsite. This is the lady's first visit to "the wilderness corridor," and she thrills at the stillness and the natural beauty which surrounds her. She has come in search of a friend and prays that he is ok.

Early each morning she sits on the rock outcrop by shore and uses field glasses to scan the lake. Of particular importance is a nearby bayou to her right where she watches for any sign of a woodsman and golden retriever fishing from a homemade green canvas canoe. Seeing no one, the woman spends the rest of her days exploring the lake from her own craft. Activities include hiking the trail to the lookout tower on the top of 1,800-foot-tall Allagash Mountain. There she picks fresh blueberries and gazes at the world below. Mesmerized by the view, she feels insignificant against the backdrop of a blue sky and acres of dark green forest, and feels sad that she left her camera in her tent.

Descending the mountain, the single paddler returns to her canoe and paddles easily across a flat-calm water to arrive at the pond's outlet. There she guides the 18-foot canoe around the remains of an old roll logging dam; a remembrance of when thousands of cords floated down tributaries and streams toward pulp, paper and lumber mills located over a hundred miles away.

Caught by the current, she quickly covers the three miles down the lake's lower stream to Little Allagash Falls. There she devours a tuna sandwich, baked potato chips and an iced tea while she studies the potholes in the blue-gray ledges worn years before, with small stones held captive in the washed-out hollows of the stone ridges. Once encased, the rocks had spun in washing machine fashion—around and around—potholing bigger and bigger cavities whenever spring floods cascaded over the outcroppings.

Returning upstream she wades against moderate flow and over shallow rips; the adventurer pulls on the canoe's bow line, drawn tight by the current, until she reaches water deep enough to paddle. Arriving back on the expanse of blue, the lady is so tired she blades the streamlined boat to an expansive sand beach on the north end. There she takes a natural sunbath— secure in the feeling that she has the whole lake to *herself*. Once refreshed, she paddles to the famous Ice Caves where Margaret descends deep into the caverns to look for any indication of etchings that may once have been scribed on the granite walls —well below ground—but she doesn't find any.

Each day before dark, Maggie arrives back at the campsite where she takes up a vigil of watching and waiting for her friend to appear. But he never does. After five days it is time to return to her desk at the Penobscot Basin Times. *Maybe*, she thinks, *my editor will allow me time to work on a book about the river. I can't help but sense that there is a much bigger story here! And it's time for me to search out Bella, and find the trunk—what could possibly be stored in that luggage?* She wonders and then considers, *I hate to leave—this would be a great place to spend the summer—writing.*

On the last night of her camping trip, the reporter makes a final trek to the 'Caves'. Standing in the opening of this ancient chasm, she removes a penny amulet threaded onto a blue cotton necklace. Margaret gently drapes the charm over a softwood root that grows centered over the cavern's entrance. Watching for a moment, but not seeing any, the lady turns to walk down the trail. Twenty feet down the path, within sight of the cave, she pauses at the base of a large standing white birch tree and, with an indelible Sharpie she carries for just such an occasion, Margaret scribes in black ink a final homage to her friend:

The Ranger and the Reporter

thinking—*perhaps if her friend Jim is still alive, maybe he'll see it?*

Tomorrow morning she'll return home and to a future husband, and wait for a son yet to be conceived. Secure in the knowledge that the lucky charm, delivered by her great uncle, will patiently wait until, someday down the road, another person will escape to the woods to retrieve the coin *for the sake of the family.* Within minutes the one-cent talisman fades invisibly into the stone over the moss-covered fissure, but the message in black ink scribed on the white birch bark remains.

Back at the Ledges Campsite, Maggie watches the campfire until the flames die. Once the hot embers turn from red to black, she walks towards the tent and to bed. From somewhere out in the lake a loon calls and the ancient bird's tremolo is promptly answered by a barred owl inquiring "who cooks for you?" Hearing the question, she softly wonders *what must it have been like for the wives of woodsmen, like Susan Clark, who lived in the remote forest with their warden and ranger husbands? How did the women handle the isolation, when their spouses were away? Did the ladies miss their moms, dads and families back home? Did they ever keep diaries about all that must have happened?* Or Margaret pondered, *was there constantly worrying over their partner returning in one piece—a greater fear?*

The stars are so bright Margaret feels like one could be plucked from the sky and put in her pocket to save for a rainy day. Crawling into her nylon shelter and wiggling into a goose down sleeping bag, the journalist sighs softly with disappointment because she hasn't found her friend. Maggie immediately falls asleep—into the deepest slumber she's had in years.

Early the next morning she awakes to the sound of a crackling fire and briefly considers making coffee; only coming fully alert when she remembers that the night before, the campfire had been fully extinguished before retiring to her tent.

Worried there might be a raging wildfire, Margaret throws off her bedding and flies out the door of the nylon shelter. Once in the open air, she is relieved to discover a small warming fire burning brightly in the site's rocked-up fireplace. Curious as to how the blaze could have possibly started, the lady walks towards the burning red.

When she passes the cedar picnic table she discovers a breakfast waiting. A pint jar of canned fiddleheads with a large brook trout rolled in cornmeal, lying on a piece of light tan birch bark, waits to be cooked. On the table, beside the morning meal, she finds a note written on the white side of a smaller piece of the "paper-like tree skin." Picking up the pastoral note, there is a message written in charcoal, by someone who'd used the small end of a burnt hardwood twig, like a pencil.

Thinking, *my the handwriting looks strangely familiar,* Margaret read;

Dear Maggie,

I hope you enjoy breakfast.
I am well and trust you are too. By the way I hear a ranger's job has opened on the lake and they will be interviewing soon.
Don't forget the trunk!
I remain fondly yours,

Stunned by this note and the early morning gifts, Margaret looks up directly towards the inlet. There she sees the distant silhouette of a person and a dog in a canoe fading into the morning fog. Looking back down at the note she rereads the last sentence **"a ranger's job has opened on the lake and they will be interviewing soon!"** Smiling, Margaret realizes that her friend is ok—but now it is time to return home, and begin the book that she promised to write. *But, if the note and treats are from Jim, why didn't he sign his name? Why didn't he stay for a visit?*

Then she realizes that once again he's mentioned the trunk. *What could possibly be in that old chest for Jim to be making such a fuss? After all the old ranger has shared, what could be left to discover?* Maggie's investigative mind could only wonder.

After devouring the delivered breakfast, the tanned lady packs her camping gear and scans the site to make sure the campfire is doused and that nothing has been left behind. Loading her canoe, she places her left foot on the cedar-planked floor of the transport and with her right, pushes off to begin the two-hour voyage upstream to her waiting vehicle. Paddling towards the inlet, Margaret takes one last look at the bogan to her left and reflects on the unexpected discovery that brought her to this place—so deep in the Maine woods. Nearing Johnson Stream, she stares at a beaver adding sticks and mud to the family's dam in the small brook, and she completely misses seeing a sloped outcropping of ledge on the opposite bank. If she had noticed the ledge, Margaret probably would still not have seen the rock shelf from which a narrow trail led to a rustic log cabin.

THE RANGER'S WIFE
THE JIM CLARK SAGA
CHAPTER 2

Gone

Our reporter's first trek to Allagash Lake began after she paid a final visit (which she did not know at the time) to Bangor's Pleasant Ridge assisted living community. Because of the *unexpected revelations learned while at the home,* Margaret's journey to the northern forest had occurred weeks sooner than expected.

On assignment, which the editor of the hometown paper had insisted she complete, Margaret Sanborn Woodward had spent hours interviewing the, at first secretive but eventually cooperative, retired ranger, Jim Clark. But now the task was nearly complete; all she had left was to edit and finalize the pre-write for the Penobscot Basin Times.

Today she has returned to ask the old woodsman a few clarifying questions; and more importantly to thank Jim for his honesty in sharing his experiences and years spent "in the bush" as the old timer had affectionately called the deep forest. Jim had been so supportive of her story that he'd even turned over his red ranger journals for her research. Now the reporter hoped to keep the outdoorsman's logs a few days longer in order to double-check her facts, if Jim would let her.

Seemingly only days before, Margaret had recovered the

1838 copper heirloom from the Cornville cemetery as Jim had instructed *under the oddest of conditions*, although she'd *be surprised if it was anything more than an interesting trinket.*[1] But since Jim had pointed the way to the family treasure, she felt compelled to wear the blue cotton necklace with the antique penny around her neck; Maggie found that the copper coinage hung comfortable against her upper chest. Despite her recovering the dangling keepsake from a cold stone slab, the metal felt strangely warm against her skin. From the moment of discovery, her life had changed.

When Margaret had called on Friday to make one more appointment, Jim had requested she come to the care facility early on the following Monday, because as he had emphasized, "I work best in the morning." Margaret was anxious to show off the charm. But when she pulled into the parking lot the reporter saw something that made her forget about the ornament. Parked in front of the double doors of the home, Margaret saw an ambulance with red and blue emergency lights flashing. She quickly pulled into her usual parking spot and found the space normally occupied by the old ranger's 4x4 truck empty.

Entering the building Margaret found a flurry of activity. Paramedics, nurses and orderlies were packing medical bags and rushing out of the building while residents gathered in small clusters and whispered in low tones.

Approaching the front desk the receptionist had looked up at Margaret. From the redness of the greeter's eyes, the reporter could tell she'd been crying. "Is Jim here?" the journalist shyly asked, unsure if she might be interrupting some sort of emergency.

The greeter waited a minute before she replied, took a deep

---

[1] Author's Note: For more information about the coin and blue ribbon that Margaret is wearing refer to Chapter 16 of Tim's book *The Ranger and the Reporter.*

breath and sniveled, "We think Jim is gone. The ambulance has taken him away and George has followed the emergency vehicle with their family truck."

Feeling like she had been slapped, Margaret couldn't believe what she was hearing. *It couldn't be true! He'd seemed so healthy at her last visit.* "What happened?" the writer asked as she felt the weight of the sadness and collapsed into a near-by chair.

"Jim's son was visiting and said his dad started complaining of chest pains and that his left arm was numb. We called the fire department and they sent an ambulance to transport him. It happened so sudden. Just yesterday he'd told some of his stories in the game room; we were all there laughing. I don't know, I just don't know. So sad, so sad!"

Despondent, Margaret rose to her feet, but her knees felt frail and she expected that her legs might crumple at any minute. Struggling to find her composure, Margaret wandered aimlessly into the day room. There the puzzle lady said to her, "We are so sorry. He spoke so well of you. Jim said you were like family. We all are going to miss him. Yes, all of us for sure!"

Margaret forced a smile and looked about the room filled with residents. She noticed that the coffee pot was empty, several types of birds had disappeared from the feeder, and a cloud blocking the sun prevented the day's warmth from flowing into the usually cheerful room. Everywhere the reporter looked there was the feeling of emptiness. Margaret felt a strange quiet which had settled like a silencing fog over the community. Residents were sitting about the day room. Those who were talking were doing so in soft whispers—out of respect for their missing friend.

Others were just sitting about and watching the few birds that remained perched outside; in nature's harmony they sang, ignoring the well-stocked feeders. Margaret thought that the melody of the winged friends seemed especially soothing today; like the sweetness of a heavenly refrain. Turning towards the entrance she saw that Jim's chair was positioned as before, only this time it was empty. Despite the room being crowded and that many people stood—no one claimed the vacant seat. After a while Margaret regained her composure and wandered down to Jim's room. The door was unlocked and she felt strangely uncomfortable entering a place where she had spent so much time. But she felt or *was it needed* to take one last visit to—*a home away from home*, she thought, *a place where I felt relaxed, safe and welcomed.*

Walking by the bathroom door into the apartment's living area, everything was still there. The pictures and award plaques on the wall, the decorated cook stove, and the stuffed deer mount gun rack. Margaret couldn't quite tell, everything seemed to be there, but yet *something was absent?*

Margaret noticed that the middle drawer to the desk was open and so she decided to close it before leaving the room. *What's missing,* she wondered as she approached the desk. Putting her hand on the drawer's handle, she noticed an envelope sitting in a place of prominence, where it would be readily seen. Preparing to push the correspondence inside the drawer, she saw bold handwriting that identified the addressee:

To Margaret Woodward

followed by the instructions,

if I am not here, please see that Ms. Woodward gets this envelope.

And it was signed

Thank you. James Paul Clark

Moving the letter, Margaret noticed there were several mostly full bottles of medicine. Reading the labels, the prescriptions were made out to Jim and were prescribed to lower cholesterol and drop his blood pressure. *If these are Jim's meds, it sure seems like he didn't take many. Wonder if that is what got him?*

He had left her a note, perhaps his final words? Margaret wondered as she caressed the handwriting to make one final connection with someone to whom she had felt so close.

Margaret tucked the envelope in her coat pocket, closed the drawer and walked toward the hall. Taking one last look at the mounted deer head, Margaret understood what had disappeared. *It was the Marlin rifle, the 38-40,* she realized. Then Margaret assumed, *probably the son took it.*

Getting into her car, Margaret didn't open the letter right off, but decided to drive back to her apartment so she could read her friend's words in privacy. She choked back the tears, and wasn't sure how much longer she could hold back the flood of sadness that consumed her body. It was like she had once again… lost her family.

Once inside her apartment and seated at her favorite spot by the window, Margaret poured an extra strong cup of coffee and opened the letter only to have a small key fall out of the envelope and bounce onto the floor by her feet. Picking up the key and holding it with her left hand, Margaret read the typed pages:

May 29th
Dear Maggie,

THIS IS FOR YOUR EYES ONLY! Please keep this message confidential.

I didn't want to leave without saying goodbye. I've only stayed at the center these many years because I was waiting for you to visit and ask about my living in the woods. I've had a good life and one that I think others might enjoy. I also hope that someday my experiences will be of interest to my family. But I needed the right person to write that story. Your editor, Mark, said you'd be the one. And as we talked I knew you were the person in the image I saw on the Ice Cave's walls so many years ago.

Now, when I was younger, I wished I'd asked my mom, dad, and grandfather about our family history. I suspect that my sons and daughter will feel the same way someday, and when that time comes, your article will be a family treasure.

I've enjoyed speaking with you these last few weeks and I wish you good luck with your career as a newspaper reporter. I am convinced you'll do well. You are very smart and I suspect you've already figured out that I am not as helpless as the nurses and others have tried to make me. It was easier to go along rather than argue and by letting them think I was feeble, it made for an easier getaway when the time came.

You may remember that early on in our conversation I told you that the old tan-colored pickup in the parking lot was nothing more than a psychological aid so that I would feel that I could always go home. The facility told me they kept the key so I wouldn't lose it. But I know they did it to prevent me from leaving. What the home doesn't know is that I've had a spare key ever since I've been here; and I have been waiting for the right moment to pack the vehicle. My son has been getting the truck ready for me and the home thinks the truck is his to keep.

Now that we've chatted, and the alder leaves are as big as a mouse's ear, it is time for me to go fishing and return to the woods where I belong. Don't try to find me because you won't be able to. But if you happen to paddle into Allagash Lake and set up camp at the Ledges campsite, don't be surprised if early in the morning and last thing before dark, you see an old gent with a golden retriever in a green canoe; catching square-tail trout from a spring hole located in a bogan south of where the inlet marries the lake.

The enclosed key is to my grandfather's trunk. The only members of my family who know about the old chest are my wife and daughter, Isabella. I never told my sons because they would have been curious enough to open it and I wanted you to be the one to find the family heirloom inside. My wife and daughter promised to respect my wishes to save the trunk for you. Isabella will tell you where it is kept. Bella can be reached by calling her cellphone. Once you open the chest, you'll understand why I saved the valuable for you.

When you are done with my treasure, keep what you need and please return the rest to my daughter. She knows what to do with the collection.

Fondly,

Jim

THE RANGER'S WIFE
THE JIM CLARK SAGA
CHAPTER 3

Return to Work

After the revelation about Jim, Margaret had completed her manuscript and electronically submitted her "Our Maine Man" document to the editor of the Penobscot Valley Times, who immediately published the work. The journalist was pleasantly surprised weeks later when, at a publisher's symposium, she had received two honors based on her submission: the first being New England's Correspondent of the Year; and the second, the prestigious American Literacy Award. The latter came with a book contract which included a $10,000 advance.

Pleased with the recognition, she'd been encouraged to travel north to look for her friend and benefactor. Margaret had spent five days on the lake; just when she thought he wouldn't show, she'd found an unsigned note, with a breakfast of brook trout and fiddleheads waiting for her. On the distant lake surface she thought she had seen the silhouette of a man and a dog in a canoe disappear into an early morning fog just as Jim's final note from the retirement community had described. Feeling somewhat relieved, but still a little unsure, Margaret was positive it was the old ranger who had left her the morning treat. Even so it was time to head home.

By the time she'd paddled halfway upstream and passed by the brook that flowed from Johnson Pond, Margaret's thoughts turned to her apartment, returning to work and her new found friend Warden Dennis James. *Yes,* she smiled reflectively *it would be nice to see Dennis again; it was so good of him to let me borrow his pick-up.* And then she remembered the book advance from the publishing company. The money should have been electronically deposited into her account by now. *She hoped the bank had sent her a statement confirming the payment. Her debit card didn't have enough balance to pay many bills.*

Once at the upper stream landing, Margaret loaded her gear into the back of her friend's pickup, and stored her personal pack on the back seat. Next the woman lifted the upside down bow of the canoe onto the racks. Once she had one end up, Margaret easily picked up the stern of the craft and slid it into place, where tie-downs secured the canoe for the seven hour trip home.

Driving slowly she watched for game. Ruffed grouse rolling in sand beside the road stared in protest at the truck that interrupted the bird's dust bath. Off to the left she just caught the flash of a white tail as a deer bounded out of sight; only to stand a few feet into the woods peeking around the trunk of a large white-birch to determine if the 4x4 presented any danger to her spotted fawn.

She almost hit a spruce grouse; the colorful dark bird with the red combs over its eyes and orange band on its tail. A cousin to the ruffed grouse, the bird's primary defense was to stiffen like a statute whenever it sensed danger; even if sitting on the dusty shoulder of a heavily traveled dirt road. The charcoal colored grouse that thought softwood spruce needles and buds were a delicacy didn't understand the harm that a seven thousand pound vehicle represented.

Margaret had concentrated so hard on avoiding the bird

that she almost hit a bull moose standing in the middle of the road. The sun reflected off the tan palms of the antlers, while the 900 pound animal with poor eye sight used his senses of hearing and smell to identify the blurry object headed his way. Margaret jammed on her brakes and the moose spun on hind legs, tilted its head slightly diagonal to avoid vertical standing timber, and ran into the forest. The reporter marveled at how easily the moose moved through the trees, despite his 48-inch spread.

When she passed Umbazookus Lake and crossed the historic Mud Pond Carry, she saw the colorful reddish-brown tail of a red-tailed hawk that hunted from a dead branch of a hardwood tree and watched for a take-out lunch. When the traveler crossed Midnight Brook on the Telos Road, a ghostly lynx, unseen and silent, faded into a fir thicket to escape the rolling dust cloud that trailed behind the half-ton truck.

Margaret paused briefly at the North Maine Woods checkpoint to turn in her road-use-pass to the attendant on the porch. While she didn't see the shadowy figure standing motionless inside, he saw her. When the reporter's vehicle eased to a stop, the visitor slowly turned in time to stare out the glass of the storm door and recognized the pretty lady behind the steering wheel.

Smiling, the 60-year-old man stared and muttered, "Well, I'll be damned—it's my old friend Maggie. I'd been thinking about seeing her again. Yup, I read about my step-daughter gettin' that award for writin' some foolishness about a lazy-good-for-nothing ole ranger, and figured she might need my help managing all that money. But not right now, got to head to Churchill and check my rope, take care of that pig's head before it starts to stink, and then off to gather a few brookies for the freezer. All needs to be done before somebody with a big nose and a rusty badge comes along."

The female gate attendant who heard the tall thin aging

customer muttering, paused in her duty of filling out the checkpoint's entrance pass, looked up and asked, "What did you say?"

"Nothing important, just talking to myself," the man known as Taut replied, glad the receptionist hadn't caught his verbalized thoughts.

"Oh ok. By the way where are you headin' today?" the smiling counter clerk patiently asked.

"Useless Road down by Telos Dam," Taunton answered but thought, *none of your damn business, nobody up here needs to know where I'm headin'.*

Taunton Scudder walked out the door of the gate house just in time to see Warden Dennis James arrive from the north and pull to a stop. The veteran warden recognized the person whom he had pursued many times. "Well, good morning to you, Mr. Scudder."

"Nothing good about it!" Taut arrogantly answered.

"Going into the woods for a few days?" the warden asked.

"Maybe I am, maybe I'm not." the sour faced man replied not interested in providing any information to the wildlife protector who had been too close on his heels way too often.

"Where you headed now?"

"Told the person in the gatehouse goin' over to the Useless Road."

Warden James knew Scudder very well, and expected the man was misdirecting. *But for what reason this time?* He thought. *Guess I'll just have to see which way he goes.*

But Taunton had to get one dig in before he dusted out of sight and said, "Looks like the State bought you a new truck? Ford is it?"

"Yup, ain't it a beaut!" the warden replied trying to at least act friendly.

Taunton jeered, "Perfect for you, because you'll have so many breakdowns that you'll spend more time walking than riding!"

With that he left the warden standing in the middle of the parking lot, and drove north. Once he was out of sight of the gate, Taunton Scudder put, as the log-hauling truckers used to say, the-pedal-to-the-metal. Warden James could look around the Useless Road and Telos Dam all he wanted, but ole Taut wouldn't be there *at least not today,* the poacher grinned, pleased he'd thrown the game warden off his trail.

But Warden James had been on the job long enough to know better than to trust the word of a man like Scudder. *Quite an insult, ole Taut gave, didn't expect I'd ever be asking him for a ride anyway.* Then smiling the Warden thought, *More than likely I'll be giving him a ride—to jail.* With that Dennis James went into the gatehouse to see who else may have entered the North Maine Woods, and where the most activity seemed to be headed.

Margaret had passed south by the intersection of the Cuxabexis Road and Telos Road just before Warden Dennis James arrived at the North Maine Woods gate. By the time Margaret crossed the Telos Bridge over the West Branch of the Penobscot River and turned left onto the Golden Road, her mind had transformed from marveling at the woods community to thinking about the routine waiting for her back at home.

Arriving back at the Bangor apartment, Margaret unloaded her personal equipment onto the porch of the boarding house and dropped the borrowed truck at Warden's James house on the other side of town. There she picked up her waiting car and returned to the place she called a temporary home.

It was good that Margaret didn't see the person or the look in the man's eye at the checkpoint. She had convinced herself that he was out of her life forever, but the female would soon learn otherwise.

When Margaret opened the door to her apartment and set down her pack on a near-by chair, and cooler on the kitchen floor, she transferred the remaining food into the refrigerator. Once all of her belongings had been stored, Margaret made a fresh pot of tea and turned to check her mail that had been deposited in her mail box at the foot of the stairs to her apartment.

Perusing through the normal statements requesting payment of her college loan, fuel bill, and credit cards, she found the receipt from the bank confirming the money for the New England Journalism and book advance had been deposited into her account. Then, at the bottom of the pile, she found a greeting-card-sized envelope that was the last thing she ever expected. With a return address of Mrs. Susan Clark of Millinocket, and wondering what that could be about, Margaret tore open the correspondence, found a cut out page from a section of the newspaper, The Penobscot Basin Times, and immediately cried...

Dear Margaret,

I hope you can join us!

Susan Clark

Penobscot Valley Times
Events page D8
James Paul Clark

Our beloved husband, father, and friend has departed and will be missed. However he is now in a better place.

For a short time, as a young man, Jim ran a farm in Cornville. But he eventually moved into the North Woods where he worked as a ranger; protecting Maine's natural resources. He loved the job and often recounted accounts about his exploits.

Known for a keen sense of humor, Jim was fond of saying that he had lived so far in the Maine woods, that no matter what direction he traveled; he was on the way to town.

Jim freely shared his appreciation for the environment and the family remembers many adventures, especially the times spent at Allagash Lake.

Jim's wife, Susan, and his children, Jim Jr., younger son George, and daughter Isabella would like you to join them in a celebration of Jim's life at the Millinocket Congregational Church on June 18th at 11 a.m.

After a brief remembrance, the congregation will adjourn outside (weather permitting) to the Church's picnic area for refreshments, anecdotes and songs by the campfire. For those who perform music, please bring your instruments and musical ability.

As Jim used to say "Happy trails to you!"

THE RANGER'S WIFE
THE JIM CLARK SAGA
CHAPTER 4

The Service

A lot of family and friends attended today's remembrance ... — Susan's Diary, May 21st.

Four days after returning home and receiving the unexpected invitation, Margaret arrived at the Church and thought, *this has got to be the saddest day ever.* As she entered the sanctuary for the first time, the correspondent paused and carefully observed her surroundings. The room was appropriately decorated for the occasion and 'filled to the brim' with people of all shapes and sizes squeezed into every pew.

Wildflowers and lilacs arranged in white ceramic vases were strategically placed so their sweet-smelling fragrances floated through open windows on the spring breeze; the room had filled quickly with pleasing aromas. Hardwood framed pictures of white, pale yellow and pink ladyslippers were hung in admiration for Maine's wild orchid; so appreciated and yet so delicate, the wildflower had been classified endangered and thus was not to be picked. Round woven wicker flower baskets filled with the edible delicacy fiddlehead fronds, were placed as a reminder of the importance of healthy eating. Margaret was somewhat surprised to see the display of blossoms because the announcement in the paper had instructed 'in lieu of flowers, please make a donation to the 'Katahdin Relay for Life' to support their campaign to fight cancer. *Did Jim have cancer?* The reporter could only wonder.

Moments before, the reporter had arrived at the enamel-white cathedral for today's ceremony. She'd found it difficult to find a parking place amidst the squadrons of four wheel drive trucks, mid-size cars, and motorcycles. There were so many vehicles; Maggie had finally squeezed her car into a narrow opening several hundred yards from the place of worship. Walking up a cobblestone walkway that cut diagonally across a forest green manicured lawn, the newcomer solemnly passed between a color guard of eight rangers and two game wardens, five on each side of the path. The rangers were attired in their forest green and gray Class A uniforms and the wardens in their green uniforms, all standing at attention. Approaching the honor guard, she was surprised to see Warden Dennis James, standing on one side, last in line. When he made eye contact the tanned woodsman man gave her a slight wink of recognition. Margaret felt her checks flush.

Margaret, normally observant of her surroundings, but today consumed by emotions, didn't see the other man watching from across the street. The tall lanky stranger stood partially hidden in the shade of a dank alley between two houses, drinking a can of cold beer and watching. Once he saw Margaret, he glared at the disappearing head of the reporter. After the funeral goer had entered the church, the outsider lit a cigarette and, despite hearing church music reminiscent of his youth, he jeered.

Once indoors among refrains of the hymn 'We come to the

garden alone...' the reporter scanned the congregation searching for a place to sit, but every pew seemed filled to capacity. Despite the crowd, the music, and the scents, heaviness draped like a cloak of sadness over the entire room.

Sunlight flowed through decorative stained glass windows ,creating an atmosphere of reverence and respect. In the front of the church, centered on a decorative white-cloth-covered oak nightstand, sat a barrel-shaped homemade cedar urn. Beside the vessel sat the portrait of a young ranger. Underneath the picture was a green and white cloth banner that displayed the name of Jim Clark, followed by the letters RIP. On the floor beside the table, on a camouflage-colored dog bed, lay a golden retriever, not sleeping, but never the less silent as if the pet understood the solemnness of the occasion. Then there was the oil painting; Margaret stared. In a place of honor on a tripod stand in front of the speaker's podium was an idyllic portrayal of a forest landscape. Quite simple, yet the color was so spectacular one would gape to absorb the beauty. In the painted scene stood a large tree with reddish brown bark and softwood boughs; the lowest limb held clustered sheaths of three pine needles and pine cones. The colors of the needles were dark forest green and the sky above the tree was painted an effervescent blue. The portrait of a woods scene was of a tall red pine—one that historic lumberjacks would have drooled over to cut down. But upon further study, other images could be found.

This was a reminder of the historical 'King's Pine,' once reserved by England for use as a mast during the pre-revolutionary war British navy. Sitting on a lower limb of the tree near a sheath of needles waited a pair of the colorful birds, the red cardinal. Both birds had triangular crests on their heads, while the male was brilliant red and the female was a pale brown with reddish tinges on the wings, tail and crest. From where Margaret stood, she couldn't tell if the painting was signed, nor understand the significance of such a beautiful work at such a solemn occasion. *Perhaps Jim or Susan had created it;* the reporter could only speculate.

Margaret, not seeing any available seating among the cushioned pews, searched for a place to stand along the left-hand wall where she could watch the proceedings. When her gaze turned toward the front of the podium, the reporter saw a woman with dark brown hair rise from the front bench near the urn, and walk towards the back of the room and directly to where Margaret Sanborn Woodward stood. Staring at the approaching person, Margaret saw a slightly older version of herself and wondered, *am I looking in a mirror? This lady could be my sister!*

Stopping in front of the reporter the woman softly whispered out of respect for the circumstances questioned, "Are you Maggie?" Margaret observing the protocol of silence, only nodded yes. "Hi," the woman said in a whisper and stuck out a white gloved hand in greeting and as they shook hands she explained, "I am Jim's youngest child, Isabella, and we've saved you a seat. Won't you join us?" Without waiting for an answer, the woman turned and Margaret obediently followed her to the first row. There Bella introduced the reporter to the old ranger's family. Jim Jr. shook her hand and said, "Nice to see you again." George smiled hello. When they reached the end of the row Bella introduced, "this is our mom, Susan." Smiling the woman met Margaret's gaze and tucked a journal type of book decorated with a bright array of flowers beside her left thigh.

Though in obvious grief, the woman looked up at Maggie's approach, stuck out her right hand and smiled and whispered, "Thank you for coming." While the mother wore a modest engagement ring and gold band on her left hand, Margaret noticed on the ring finger of Susan's right hand was another piece of jewelry which framed a black stone. Obviously a man's ring had been wrapped with yarn so it would stay on the woman's smaller digit. Peppered through the gem were hints of red flecks. Susan, dressed in black for the occasion, had short black hair sprinkled lightly with gray, and a trim physique obviously used to being outdoors. Her sun-tanned skin only served to highlight the clearest deepest emerald eyes that Margaret had ever seen. In her lap Susan tightly held two books, one on top of the other. The first was a black leather covered Bible; a large tome, which concealed the second publication.

The reporter took the seat beside Jim's wife while the minister strode to the podium to begin today's ceremony. The golden retriever looked at the parson to determine if there was any danger. Sensing none, the dog sighed and lowered her chin onto her front paws. The preacher began speaking while the heavenly music faded. "Welcome family to today's celebration of the life and times of James Paul Clark. Notice I didn't say welcome to family and friends and that wasn't an oversight." Here a small murmur rose through the crowd as if the sardine packed room was unsure of how welcome they were to be there. The minister continued, "I said 'family' because that is how Jim and Susan consider each and every one here. On several occasions when I visited him at the Pleasant Ridge community, he would share a story about members of his 'extended family' and talk with pride about the good times and shared achievements." Here the audience grinned at the recognized bond and closeness each had felt whenever they had spent time with Jim and his family, regardless if they were at his home, or he in theirs.

"The Clark family appreciates your support and wants everyone to know that this is not a time for sadness, but a time for rejoicing of life, and an existence that touched many with humor, sensibility, and respect of Maine's natural world. Jim hasn't left us—he's just relocated. Many of you may be aware, that during his stay in the woods, Jim often wrote poetry. I read many of his pieces, and while he humorously called it his 'fracture rhymes,' I always found the stanzas down to earth with an everyday message based on personal experiences.

"With that in mind, for today's invocation I would like to read one of Jim's verses. According to Susan, Jim wrote this elegy one night after spending the day recovering the bodies of two fishermen from Eagle Lake. While on their annual spring fishing trip the victims who weren't wearing their life jackets, went overboard after a northwest gale caused their canoe to capsize. The official report noted that most likely, once in the cold water the men were overcome by hypothermia and then lost. Later that same day, Jim found the submerged craft and the search and rescue continued until the bodies were recovered two days later. Saddened by yet another tragedy, that night while thinking about the preciousness of life, Jim scribed these lines. Let us pray.

"Going Home"

God works in mysterious ways;
At least that is what we've been told.
So what happens when we leave this world?
When we move beyond being old?
Will I find the River Jordan?
And experience a baptismal submerse?
Or will I see a light at the end of a tunnel,
a bridge that must be traversed?

Will I ascend a glistening staircase?

That holds a light from beyond
Where I'll be greeted by loved ones
And a Golden Retriever will bond.
Yet.
I don't expect to see my God
Sitting on a Golden Throne,
But to be greeted by a humble Shepard
Bringing His flock home.
There is so much to life;
And abundance which has been done,
There must be more to give
After my earthly days are run.
So I'll put my trust in Jesus
And my future in his hands,
And will trust my faith
Has not been built on sand.
When all is said and all is done,
where may I go?
I guess the proper answered is'
"only heaven knows".

—Ranger Jim Clark
One night at my cabin

After the brief invocation the minister then turned and said, "Now is the time for testimony, first I would like to introduce Jim's wife of 48 years, Susan Clark."

The woman beside Margaret rose leaving the books on her seat, smoothed her black dress and strode with confidence toward the podium while the preacher took a seat nearby. Their dog, Sandi, looked up and wagged her tail at the mother's approach. But the canine didn't offer to leave her post. Susan crouched for a second to scratch the pet's ear, and with a raised palm facing the dog, Susan reminded the family pet to stay, and turned to stand behind the lectern. The wife took a deep breath to become calm and then spoke in a loud clear unwavering voice. Margaret looked down at the book and saw a brown leather-covered journal with the words "Susan's Diary" embossed in gold.

"Welcome to everyone! My children and I are pleased you were able to join us on this celebration of our loved one. In preparation for today I wondered what I should speak about. Should I mention the numerous people that we have encountered on our journey? But I was afraid I would forget someone and I didn't want to do that, so I have decided to speak about my life with Jim.

"Whoever would believe that a girl born in Waterbury, Connecticut who moved to Millinocket and a boy born in Cornville, Maine would eventually get together; yet our paths crisscrossed at an early age. Soothsayers might say we were predestined to be together.

"Our close encounters started at an early age. When I was in grade school, a number of families from Millinocket would camp at Abol Campground in Baxter State Park. We kids were always bugging the local ranger and that ranger was Jim's uncle, Buzz. To make a long story short, Ranger Buzz mentioned that he milked a moose every morning so we called his bluff. One morning we all tramped down to the ranger's log

cabin to see if the ranger did indeed milk a moose."[2] It took several minutes for Susan to finish one of the family's favorite tales with, "although we never talked, that is probably the first time that my husband and I met.

"Of course we probably crossed paths again at Katahdin Stream and Russell Pond campground, because I often camped there while Jim stayed many nights with his uncle, Aunt Jan and their daughters, Cathy and Tammy.

"During the early 1970s, I worked at Togue Pond gate in the Park. Uncle Buzz was my boss. When he learned that I was going to the University of Maine at Machias, Buzz suggested that I look up his nephew Jim. At the time I wasn't interested and so I brushed him off. But every time I came home from college he would ask, "Have you seen Jim?"'

"So I decided I'd better look up Jim just to, if nothing else, shut Buzz up. Little did I know what that would lead to! So one day I asked a girl in my business class if she knew this Jim Clark, and if she did, would she introduce me. A couple of days later in the University's cafeteria, there he was. Before I could escape we were being introduced. That night he called and asked me for a date. What a romantic first night out.

"We strolled leisurely down O'Brien Hill into Machias and to the local Colonial Theater. The movie playing that night was Disney's 'Son of Flubber!' From that first date our romance eventually blossomed, although initially, our attempts at dating seemed more like skirmishes than outings.

"One day in June we were walking along the shores of Abol Pond, Jim proposed to me. Excited, we couldn't wait to tell our families the good news. Their response should have sent a message because Jim's mother cried and mine threw up." Here Susan paused and smiled reflectively as she remembered the year and explained that at the time of their announcement her mom suffered from the flu.

"On April 15th (the day when Federal income tax is due, the Titanic

---

[2] Author's note: For the complete 'Milking the Moose' tale see Allagash Tails Volume V *Headin North.*

sunk and Abraham Lincoln passed) we were married in Millinocket and started our journey as a couple. We have lived in State Parks like Aroostook and Cobscook, the Allagash, and finally we bought a house in my home town of Millinocket.

"As I reminisce, I think of places where we swam in sparkling waters, snorkeling in the Caribbean, where we traced the routes of Black Beard the pirate; sitting in a mineral spa in a small town in Colorado where Wyatt Earp's friend Doc Holiday spent his final days. We waded in rivers that Lewis and Clark boated, and swam in a favorite swimming hole known as 'Cindy and Pete' in Katahdin Stream with the Yeti of Baxter Park.

"Ah, but you say there is no such thing as a Yeti. But au contraire, I say there is. The summer after Jim's retirement from his ranger job is also the year that he decided to grow a beard. Although he was quite proud of his facial liberation, the whiskers were multi-colored and quite bushy. That is also the time that Jim and I decided we were going to look for one of my favorite haunts as a young girl scout at Camp Natarswi—'Cindy and Pete,' a small set of granite falls where we could slide down smooth granite into a cool pool of water. Jim had talked with Baxter Park rangers and they had told him the hiking route to follow. Finally after exploring several small falls we came to a smooth outcropping of rocks that we thought must be the sought after swimming hole.

"But so much had changed. A few years before, a forest fire had completely transformed the scenery and thus drastically altered the landscape from when we were young. It was an extremely hot day and so around noon we looked around and thought that nobody else would be as crazy as us to go on a hike on a 100-degree day, in the open sunlight. So we decided to take a swim au naturel.

"As we were splashing about and discussing the brilliant views Mountain Katahdin on the horizon, something caught my eye. You guessed it. I could see two heads bobbing up and down and heading directly towards us. I scurried into the bushes and Jim hid behind a bunch of highbush blueberries, shirtless, multi-colored beard, tangled hair and all. As the man and woman neared shore, with chest exposed, Jim popped up,

*raised the index finger on his right hand to get their attention and said in a firm voice, "'**Excuse me. Excuse me!**'" You should have seen the looks on their faces. Their eyes got as big as saucers and the couple stood in horror staring at this near-naked man, with a full growth of face hair, miles from any car or campground. The next thing we knew, the hikers had spun and headed on a dead run back up the trail from whence they'd come. And so you see, to those two visitors there is such a thing as the Yeti of Cindy and Pete.*

Despite the solemnness, the congregation couldn't help but laugh at Susan's remembrance.

"The high point of our life together was the birth of each of our three children: Jim Junior, George, and our youngest child, Isabella. We were so excited when each one was brought into the world. My parents traveled miles to the hospital in Presque Isle when our daughter was born. At 11 o'clock on an October night Jim called the motel room of my parents to announce the birth of the highly-anticipated granddaughter. My dad asked the typical questions "Are mother and daughter ok? What's her name? How big is she? What color is her hair? Is she pretty?" Trying to keep a stressful time light, Jim replied, "'Homer, I could have whittled a better-looking baby'" "'Well, you can imagine that did not set well with my parents and they reminded Jim about his poorly timed joke for years to come."

Here Susan paused to once again allow the prattle of laughter to spread across the room, then continued.

"Through the years, when not living in the woods we delighted to show off the history of our country to our children. Apparently after one such trip where we had seen one fort, museum, and historic park after another, 12 year old Bella turned to her dad and said, "'if we have to look at one more old thing, I am going to scream!'"

"Before we knew it, Jim had retired after 40 years of service and I after 25 years as a regional secretary for the Department of Conservation. But our explorations continued and folks never knew where they would see us: walking the beach at Roque Bluffs State Park in Washington County; canoeing down Upper Allagash Stream as we sought to discover one more

fishing hole; hiking childhood paths into Wassataquok Lake in Baxter Park where we reminisced how close we had been as children; or even strolling down Weirs Beach, a New Hampshire landmark near Jim's grandfather's house. You can be sure that wherever we went, you were in our thoughts as we mailed postcards and shared stories with family and extended family, and dreamed of the adventures and good times to come.

"No, today is not a time of sadness, but a time to rejoice in our memories and to remember the special relationships we all share. Jim is not here in body, but in spirit, and he has gone to a better place—a pleasant location where the fish are biting, and at night mosquitos can be heard humming around the light of his Coleman lantern; a paradise where the deep hooting voice of the great horned owl hollers in the distance — 'who, who' *— and where late at night the call of the common loon predicts the weather. Today is not a time for sadness, but an opportunity to recall life, celebrate friendships and recollections, and appreciate each other with gratitude. Thank you for coming."*

Despite the solemnness of the moment, the congregation was so moved by the words of Jim's wife, that they gave Susan a standing ovation.

Here Susan left the podium and reclaimed the book and seat beside her family, while the minister returned to his position usually reserved for Sunday sermons. Once the applause had dimmed, he said "Thank you, Susan, for that excellent testimony." The pastor then said, "Now is the time for anyone who might like to offer a few words. Does anyone have anything they would like to say?" Immediately a flood of hands went into the air.

While account after account provided witness to a lifetime of experiences, many rangers, guides, wardens, landowner foresters, sporting camp operators, and others waited for their turn to speak of their memories. One would start with "I remember the time that Thoroughfare Brook was swollen by a flash flood, when Jim and I rescued a car that had drowned out on the wooden bridge, with a father, ten-year-old son and wife inside…"

Then another would rise and offer, "It was during a forest fire and one of the fighters had experienced a heart attack and a helicopter pilot…"

One story would finish and immediately be replaced by another "One day Jim and I received a report of a dead body in the river below Sweeney Brook. We traveled for hours searching, reaching, hoping for a false alarm when suddenly Jim announced, "'I see the skeleton, and thank goodness, it's not from a person but the skeleton of a black bear.'" "Yes, a bear's demise had been seen in the river, and we were greatly relieved."

And the stories continued… Susan had heard them all before so she couldn't help but let her mind wander, back to another time when she was very young, recalling her first diary entry, a daily habit of scribing memories that would stay with the woman the rest of her life.

THE RANGER'S WIFE
THE JIM CLARK SAGA
CHAPTER 5

Deadheads and Mr. Moose

This morning Harold and I saw Mr. Moose... — Susan's Diary, June 8th

Young Susan scribed in her new journal one night, before bed, during a time when as a child she often stayed on Ambajejus Lake with her river-driver grandfather and boomhouse cook grandmother. Susan's mom had given the daughter a brand new pink princess diary to encourage their only child to share her adventures when the youth returned to their house in Millinocket. Decorated with a white unicorn outlined with sparkles, the little girl couldn't wait to make her first entry about an experience she had while riding in a boat with her gramps.

"Susan! Susan! I thought I told you to watch for deadheads." The grandfather yelled to the five-year-old girl seated in the bow. Speaking loudly to be heard over the roar of the river-driver's outboard motor which, even under full power, was straining to move the aluminum craft forward against the swelling waves of the lake. With a quick sideways throw of the motor's throttle handle, the 16-foot boomboat swerved sharply to the right, narrowly missing the partially exposed butt of a 20-foot-long spruce log, a piece of timber so heavy, that only a small portion of the magnificent tree's butt broke through the surface of the blue water.

Harold Kidney, Susan's grandfather
Photographs from the T. Caverly Collection

The five-year-old girl froze in her seat and scanned the foaming water, vigilant per her Pépé's instructions, yet terrified she'd see decapitated portions of body parts or worse, the vacant eyes of floating skulls. "But Harold," the little girl replied to her gramps "I don't see anybody's head."

Oh, no, the girl took me literally, thought the grandfather. *Guess I should have better explained what to look for—an obstacle so dangerous that it will upset a boat and ruin an outboard motor quicker than scat. I am gonna catch what-for when Susan tells Grammy about this one.*

Susan was the granddaughter of Harold and Elsie. Harold was a river-driver foreman for Great Northern Paper, in charge of a section of the West Branch of the Penobscot from Hopkins Pitch to Ambajejus Lake, and he lived with his wife Elsie.

The couple lived at the company's boomhouse located at the inlet where the Penobscot River married Ambejejus Lake. One month earlier, the regular camp cook had gone to town and hadn't returned. Desperate to feed his always hungry river-driving crew, Harold had asked his wife to assume the role of ensuring the men were provided with plenty of hot, nourishing food. With that invitation Elsie became the first female cook for Great Northern Paper, a role previously reserved for men. So, the deadhead situation wasn't the first time Harold had gotten in a mess with his wife.

Susan lived with her parents ten miles away in Millinocket and Harold enjoyed the little girl's visits as often as possible. Sometimes Susan would spend time with her grandparents and when she couldn't, Harold would call whenever possible. He liked having the little girl around and so when he got to a GNP wooden wall-mounted crank phone, he would call Susan and tell her about an adventure. One day he called the little girl and when he heard the small voice answer hello he said, "Hello Susan, its Harold."

"Hi Harold," the little girl said smiling to receive a call from her Nana's husband.

"Guess who I saw today?" he asked.

"Who?" the child cradled the receiver and stared at the phone base on the wall, wide-eyed and anxious to hear.

"Mr. Moose," the grandfather replied with a grin the girl couldn't see.

Elsie Kidney, grandmother of Susan King Caverly
Photographs from the T. Caverly Collection

"Did he talk to you?" the child inquired almost too excited to stand still.

"Yes and he asked when you were coming up to visit?"

Susan still holding onto the phone's receiver turned to her mother drinking coffee at the family's kitchen table and asked, "When can I go and stay with Harold and Nana?" Placing a small hand over the mouthpiece of the phone, the child added emphasis to her request and whispered, "I think they need my help."

Early the next morning Susan's parents dropped the little girl off at the boat dock on the Ambejejus side of the dike that separated Ambejejus and Millinocket Lakes. Harold was already waiting, with a soft northwest breeze promising good weather. Soon the river-driver's boat was under power, and with wind blowing through the girl's hair, the grandfather loudly announced "Elsie has molasses cookies waiting." The aluminum boat cut cleanly through the waves, carrying Susan to her favorite home away from home.

After a glass of milk and a cookie Harold asked, "I have to go to Passamagamet Lake to check the trip boom, do you want to go?"

Grinning and whipping the milk from her upper lip, Susan immediately answered "Yes." Then Elsie said, "I'm caught up on my chores, do you mind if I go too?" Susan and Harold agreed Elsie could accompany the duo.

Traveling up the river a short ways from the river-driver's camp Susan saw a moose descend from the bank of the river. Excitedly the granddaughter pointed at the animal and shouted to Harold, "There's Mister Moose!" Leaning over the side of the boat, the little girl hollered, "Mister Moose, Mister Moose, come here, I need to talk with you!" Harold grinned at the antics of the little girl, at least until she had leaned so far over the side that the child was in danger of falling overboard. Grabbing her by the collar of her coat, Harold pulled his granddaughter back into the craft just as the moose exited the river on the opposite shore.

Susan turned to her grandmother and angrily accused in her stern little girl voice, "It's all your fault! If you hadn't been here, Mr. Moose would have talked to me and Harold. You scared him off."

If looks could kill, Harold would have been mortally wounded. Elsie shot daggers at her husband, and Harold was never allowed to talk about Mr. Moose again.

THE RANGER'S WIFE
THE JIM CLARK SAGA
CHAPTER 6

After the Service

Our family witnessed an amazing amount of talent yesterday ... — Susan's Diary, May 22nd.

After 45 minutes of testimony from the congregation, the minister made the following announcement, "Thank you, everyone, for sharing your kind words and remembrances. I enjoyed hearing the stories and know the family did also. I've just been told that refreshments are ready, so we will now dismiss to tents and picnic tables set up outside of the rectory. There are picnic tables, benches, and a fire pit, for those who wish to continue their conversation around a campfire. Everyone is welcome to stay as long as they want. And," here the minister had to make one more solemn pronouncement. "According to family wishes, there will not be a grave side ceremony today, but the family will come together in a few days in a few days for a private remembrance."

The congregation filed out and as the family readied to connect with the others gathering outside, Bella asked

Margaret, "Are you joining us?"

"In a few minutes," the reporter replied. Still uncomfortable about the letter she had found the day Jim had been taken by ambulance, the reporter was not really sure if there were cremation remains inside the urn, and she needed to satisfy her curiosity.

Bella said, "Ok, but please join us—you, Mom, and I need to talk, not today but tomorrow perhaps, if you are free?" Then Bella called, "Come Sandi, Susan has a biscuit waiting for you." With that the faithful companion reluctantly left her post near the nightstand and followed her master's daughter.

After the church had emptied, Margaret remained behind to spend a few minutes of quiet time with a friend who had seemed more like family. Walking slowly to the main stage, she placed a hand on the oak display counter. Not sure why, but something she felt rather than thought required her to look inside for one last farewell to someone to whom she felt so close. On top of the barrel was a carved impression of a ranger's badge inscribed into the wood.

Noticing the lid of the miniature cask hadn't been sealed with the normal silicone epoxy, she undid the cover. Expecting to see gray ashes of a cremated body she found something totally unexpected at such an emotional time. There weren't any ashes of any kind. The cedar cask was practically empty, except for a plastic box of multi-colored trout flies, and an oddly shaped black mass with a hard cracked exterior that was about the size of a man's fist; an object that had a burnt charcoal appearance lying isolated at the bottom. *Why aren't there ashes? Why are the fishing flies in there? And what in the world is that disgusting looking fungus? Something seems awfully wrong.*

Margaret couldn't see the interior of the black lump, but if she could peer inside the chunk, which she supposed was organic, she'd have fund an interior that was rusty yellow brown in color. Beneath the growth was a small folded slip of paper addressed *To Margaret*.

When she opened the single piece of paper, Margaret found only the words **'Go to back'** typed in Ariel Black script.

Stunned, Margaret walked up the carpeted aisle, deep in thought about what it could all mean. *Go where? Allagash Lake, Allagash Mountain, the woods?* She wondered, *but why? The retirement community, her apartmen*t, or…? She couldn't even guess. When she passed into the coat room, she found Susan and Sandi waiting.

Susan slipped her arm into Margaret's, smiled and said, "I'll walk with you." Passing outside to join the crowd already gathered at the buffet table Margaret hesitantly stated, "There's, there aren't any ashes!"

"I know," Susan said and continued, "We'll talk tomorrow. For now let's join our guests. Yes, tomorrow's the best day," Susan said softy in a tone more to convince herself than her walking companion.

For her whole life Susan had been a part of, involved in and worked around a social lifestyle—from sharing a supper table with river-drivers, to ushering at high school basketball games, singing in a choir at college, to years as an information clerk in Baxter State Park and as a Maine state park receptionist, eventually promoted to become a regional secretary. Yes, for years Susan had been on the front lines of meeting and greeting, yet in her own mind she was still a private person, with hopes, fears and doubts she considered too personal; most likely a belief the daughter learned early on from her parents who stressed that it was never ok to air dirty laundry.

Susan knew some of what Jim wanted Margaret to have, but certainly not everything. For some reason he had been very secretive in describing all that was in the hardwood case, and he had asked her not to riffle through the contents. She trusted her husband because he'd never given her any cause to be suspicious. And yes, Susan fully understood her ranger-husband's belief that in the best interest of preserving and protecting Maine natural resources, sometimes skunks had to be driven out of the woodpile, but today this public lady still felt guarded.

Before the two could join the others on the church's common ground, Susan was stopped by Sandi dog straining against the leash. Pulling hard, the dog was staring at something across the street, and uttered a low growl. Between two buildings — Margaret couldn't be sure — but she thought she saw a whispery form fading out of the light—deeper into a shadowy darkness. At the same time, and it may have been Susan's imagination, but the black ring on her right finger seemed to quiver ever-so-softly, as if an invisible shifty force was at hand.

Outside, the family gathered at a hand-carved cedar bench near a comforting campfire, while others broke out musical instruments. Friends stood in a buffet line to receive their helpings of food from platters sitting on red and white checkered table cloths. Following Susan to the food table, Margaret grabbed a plate for food when she heard a familiar voice say, "It's good to see you. I've been meaning to call." Without turning around Margaret, smiled and answered, "I was hoping you would." Sensing a nearby scent of insect repellent, without turning she knew who had spoken.

In the background of the green landscape, a solitary musician crooned a modified version of a popular country song "My heroes have always been Rangers…"

Through the Crest of the Red Cardinal

A bulletin about the families of the northern forest

Sometimes finding enough to eat is quite a chore

WOODS WIFE FINDS CREATIVE WAYS TO FEED HUNGRY CREWS

When it is sixty miles to the nearest store; strategic planning is a necessity.
T10R12, Maine June (PVT)

Unexpected Guests for Dinner
by Susan Clark
Allagash Wilderness Waterway
Special to the Red Cardinal News

Spending years living in the woods as a child, and then as wife of a Maine Park Ranger, I became accustomed to dooryard visitors, pop-in's and overnight guests. Those who often stopped included co-workers, friends, timber company personnel, as well as game wardens and forest rangers. Then there was the occasional hypothermic party who had capsized in cold water and needed to warm in our camp. Not to mention the stream of VIP's passing through our door on yearly inspection trips.

Since grocery stores were a great distance from our home, I learned early on the importance of planning for meals. Both my grandmother and mom were woods women. My gran was a cook in a Great Northern Paper Company logging camp, and my mother was a Baxter Park Gate attendant who lived at the High Adventure Matagamon Boy Scout Base. Since we never knew who or when we'd have company, our pantry was kept full of coffee and sweets, because a quick run to town over rough gravel roads was not a luxury. Also it did not take the members of the woods community long to learn where there was always a hot cup of coffee.

Due to the limited capacity of our propane refrigerators, we always kept a stock of non-perishables handy, such things as canned and instant potatoes, canned vegetables, dried beans, canned meats (bacon, chicken, ham and the ever popular Spam.) We also maintained a good supply of dry and evaporated milk and powdered eggs, along with traditional baking supplies and plenty of homemade maple syrup. We weren't too concerned with what we ate, just thankful we had food.

Author's Note: Article complements of Susan King Caverly

I was often reminded of the importance of planning ahead, such as one occurrence in 1988. At the time, a wildfire named the Harrow Lake Fire in T10R12 brought a flood of people into the deep woods. Our Churchill Dam home became control central. During that containment, we accommodated 21 overnight fire fighters in an AWW headquarters designed to sleep 10.

Caused by lightning and fanned by heavy winds, the blaze eventually grew to 200 acres. First responders, helicopter crews and administrative bookkeepers were coming and going day and night. I was even hired by the Maine Forest Service to work on their support team, a job which offered long hours and little sleep, some nights only getting four or five hours rest.

During calmer times, if we couldn't get to a town in Maine and company arrived, I would make an emergency fifty mile trip to Quebec province, or if the roads had washed out, I might raid a fellow ranger's freezer. While cooking creatively was a necessity, my Great Northern cook grandmother had taught there is always room for one more at the table.

In the end, everyone always got fed but it didn't take long to learn that I needed to stay prepared. So, our standard invitation was, "Coffees on Neighbor, and perhaps a cookie or two."

THE RANGER'S WIFE
THE JIM CLARK SAGA
CHAPTER 7

You May Call Me Warden James

Dennis James was a Maine Game Warden. It's not just a job, but also a hobby; an occupation where he sometimes acted as disciplinarian, arbitrator, and protector. But the part of the job he liked best was as an educator. Afield he loved to talk with young and old to explain the marvels of nature's handiwork. It wasn't that he didn't like arresting poachers—he'd handle them persuasively whenever necessary. Through experience and intuition he could often tell when law breakers were creating intentional acts, but if he thought a minor law violation was an honest mistake—then he let them off with a warning—at least the first time.

Dennis had spent his whole life in the northern forest; it was ground where he had walked and felt the most comfortable. In another time or place or under different circumstances, Dennis might have ended up in an eight-to-five job doing piece work in a dingy factory that created little opportunity for creativity. But, it was his destiny to do other things—something recognized early on by his Grandfather, Dalton James who many affectionately nicknamed DJ.

Growing up in Bangor, his high school classmates were always trying to get him to hang out in the streets after class. Then one day the English instructor had assigned her students to bring in, for her approval, the book that they planned to read for a book report. Dennis had panicked. The teenage boy hated reading and hadn't planned on doing any more than necessary in order to squeak by. But that night his grandfather, Dalton James, had noticed the sorrowful look on the boy's face and when questioned, Dennis had explained that he was being forced to read.

DJ had suggested the book "Wilderness Warden" by Edward C. James, based on the fictional character of Warden Dan Hubbard. It was with that story, and his grandfather's guidance, on which Dennis's future hung.

Grandfather Dalton James had spent his whole life in the Maine outdoors. If all of Dalton's accomplishments could be listed (an almost impossible task), we'd learn that he'd been a trapper, hunter, guide, sporting camp operator, and for a short time a forester measuring plots for a northern Maine paper mill. After measuring plot after plot and watching many turn into clear-cuts (ground which provided little cold weather shelter to Maine's wildlife), DJ decided it was time to change jobs. He applied and was hired and became an Allagash Ranger. If there was one thing about Dalton James that was certain it was that he knew the ways of the woods, and that experience was passed along to his grandson at a very early age.

By the time Dennis turned twenty-one he'd completed the application to be a Maine Game Warden. He passed the Oral Board, although the experienced wardens who made up the interview committee tried to trip him up by asking the two-edged question, "If you are watching a fisherman should you wait for him to violate the law or make your presence known before he catches over his limit?" Dennis had answered, "I believe that I should wait for a violation to occur before stepping out." Another interviewer then asked with an accusing tone, "Don't you care about our natural resources or that some people will waste our fish and game?"

"Yes, of course, but it depends if I know the fisherman to be a habitual offender." Then Dennis had explained, "From my understanding, it is the policy of the Maine Warden Service to maintain a wait-and-see approach to intentional violators. But if it's a family out for a day of sporting, I will show myself to encourage wise use of our wildlife and to provide the sons and daughters with a positive experience."

Overall the Board remained stone-faced, showing little emotion, although Dennis thought he saw unintentional smiles creep across the face of a couple of the older wardens.

The next step was to take the polygraph or lie detector test. He hated the questions that explored the deepest part of his thoughts and habits. Walking out after the test, he'd been convinced there wasn't any part of his mental condition that the state didn't know. Then there was the psychological exam and finally the physical. Dennis didn't know it, but he had flown through the hiring process with flying colors. Then after completing a second oral board, the lieutenant in charge handed Dennis an empty manila envelope with instructions to deliver it to the Colonel at the Augusta headquarters.

The empty envelope was a signal that Dennis James had passed all the examinations and that he met the qualifications to be hired. That same day, with a raise of his right hand, Warden James had sworn to enforce laws of the State of Maine and to protect the State's fish and game. Shortly after completing warden school, Dennis began his first patrol that encompassed one of the largest districts in the North Woods.

Before long Warden James had a run-in with Taunton Scudder.

The day had started fairly calm. He checked a few fishermen catching salmon from the Big Eddy on the West

Branch of the Penobscot River. Finding their licenses and limits in proper order, he then checked boaters on Chescuncook Lake for registrations and having the proper amount of useable lifejackets.

Driving up the Telos Road, Dennis rounded a sharp curve only to see a poorly dressed man pull a large black plastic bag from the back of his truck and throw it up and over a horizontal fir tree that had blown down across an old skidder trail. Getting into the truck the thin man began to drive off. Speeding up with blue lights activated the warden caught up and pulled the vehicle over.

Carefully approaching the truck, as taught by Academy instructors, Warden James rested his right hand on the state-issued 9mm Sig Sauer Model 226 sidearm. The self-protection weapon that protected game wardens, with 12 bullets in the gun backed by 37 rounds in the magazine pouch handily carried on their duty belts.

The occupant sat unmoving behind the steering wheel, with the engine idling. As Dennis drew closer to the open window, he heard the man sniff and utter, "Wonder what that smell is? Something sure smells sour. Oh, hi, Mister Fish Cop," the man coldly said.

"You may call me Warden James. I noticed that you threw a bag into the woods. What's in it?"

"Don't know what you're talking about."

"Oh, so that's how it's gonna be," Dennis James answered, not feeling the least bit intimidated.

With a firm voice James began again, "We can do this the hard way, or the easy way. It's your choice. We can stay here all day if we need to. Now I'm gonna ask again, and just so I am clear, I expect a civil answer. But first I need your driver's license for proper identification!"

Seeing that the Warden meant business, and knowing he had miles to go before he could sleep, the operator pulled out his driver's license and handed it to the officer. After all, it was the practical thing to do. Grasping the plastic card, Warden James read the name Taunton Scudder.

"What's in the bag and why did you throw it into the woods?"

"Just a bunch of garbage," Scudder replied bluntly.

"Littering is against the law; let's go take a look."

Realizing the game warden wasn't going to quit with his questioning, Taunton decided to change his tactic. "Aw, Warden, it's just some stinky spoiled things from the refrigerator, that was smellin' up my truck. Don't give me a summons, and I'll pick up the bag and pay the fine without a fuss," Taunton hopefully suggested. After all, it wouldn't do well for the warden to look at the contents in the bag.

Not buying Scudder's sudden change in attitude Dennis ordered, "You are to go with me so I can make sure household garbage is the *only* thing in the plastic sack."

Back at the scene, Warden James grabbed an empty five-gallon plastic bucket from the bed of his truck and he and Scudder walked back to the garbage bag. Instructing Taunton to take a seat on a nearby stump, he kept a sharp eye on him to watch for any sign of movement. Opening the rubbish bag, a mixed smell of spoiled milk and rotten meat immediately met the warden's senses. Dumping the contents into the empty pail, Dennis saw that underneath the household rubbish were the remnants of over a dozen heads of brook trout, mixed among odds and ends of land-locked salmon.

Even after being threatened with jail, Taunton wouldn't admit to catching over the limits of trout and salmon from nearby Chescuncook Lake. He said they were a combination of catches over several days. To try and get away from the Warden as soon as possible, Taut promised Warden James he wouldn't give him any further trouble. Issuing a summons for littering and promptly reading him the riot act, Warden James was proving to Scudder that he was aware of his shenanigans and that he would be watched.

It had suddenly dawned on Scudder that he didn't need the Warden to search his truck and discover the loaded weapon in the glove box, the fresh deer steak in the little cooler under the seat, or the open bottle of beer. Pretending a meekness that he didn't really feel, Scudder quietly accepted the invitation to court, with a low-voiced "thank you."

Warden Dennis James and Mr. Taunton Scudder had formally met.

Through the Crest of the Red Cardinal

A bulletin about the families of the northern forest

Smoke signals a bit of drama for the Beetle Mountain watchman back in August 1935

FIRE SET BY WOMAN
TO CALL AID TO MAN

Maine Lookout Investigates; Discovery Results
Augusta, Maine Aug 15 (AP)

Oscar Perry of Presque Isle probably owes his life to the presence of mind of his wife, who set a forest fire which the watchful eyes of a fire lookout spotted from a mountain perch.

Perry went into the woods near Haymock Lake in the Allagash region, leaving his wife on the shore, Forest Commissioner Neil L. Violette said he learned today.

After Perry had been gone for many hours, Mrs. Perry started a fire, which was seen by Leon Chamberlain, a fire lookout on Beetle Mountain. He came down the mountain to investigate and found Mrs. Perry.

A search revealed Perry injured, apparently by felling a tree, far in the woods. Chief Al Thibodeau summoned aviator Jerry Smead from Greenville, and the Perrys were flown to their home.

Author's Note: Article complements of Forest Fire
Lookout Association of Maine

THE RANGER'S WIFE
THE JIM CLARK SAGA
CHAPTER 8

Taunton Scudder
"Just a natural born lollygagger"

Taunton Scudder's world was best described as turbulent. He arrived one cold March day in a room with little heat. Outside, the afternoon skies were a gloomy dark gray; colors that hinted at the predicted freezing rain. It was the type of day for those at home to lie on the couch and catch forty winks; a catnap often encouraged by the radiant warmth of a crackling fireplace.

But in the hospital's cool birthing room, the newborn was naked and screaming. He'd felt comfortable in his mother's womb and hadn't any desire to leave. But the pregnant juvenile carrying the overdue offspring was sick to death of her pregnancy—it was time for the boy to depart. *Nope, no question about it!*

Not only was the young mother in a hurry to discard the weight she'd carried for months. She was bitter about the coming child—so hostile that even during the pain of childbirth—the woman, too young to create a family, swore under-her-breath at the high school classmate who'd caused the condition—a pregnancy she didn't need nor ever want again.

At the time of conception, the father of the newborn had been a handsome senior in their local high school, and she an insecure junior. They had joined one warm spring night on an overlook locally known as Blueberry Knoll. The music played softly on the car's radio and a full moon created a hypnotic effect. But after receiving the news, the boy ditched the expectant girl and she never heard from him again. The seventeen-year-old had wanted to abort the fetus but bent to pressure of a nosy neighbor and a minister who insisted she should acquiesce to keep the baby, because as the pastor had argued, 'it must be God's will.'

Eighteen years before, the new mother had been created by an alcoholic woman and a drug-induced father, habits that ensured the girl wouldn't have a fair start in life. Randomly abused by both parents, physically and mentally, the only thing the co-ed knew was cruelty.

In school the pretty seventeen year old flirted with the most popular boys on the basketball team to show everyone that she could do and get whatever she wanted. And, after returning from court appointed counseling one day, the teenager confessed to another that she loathed the medicine that treated her Attention Deficit Hyperactivity Disorder—a defiance that didn't improve an already bad attitude. At the time, psychologists had shaken their heads in disappointment at the girl's refusal to listen to or heed their advice, and described their patient as "refusing to own her ADHD." The new mom just didn't care if the prescription was intended to help her stay focused; as far as she was concerned there wasn't anything in the world to stay motivated for. Any rate, the adolescent certainly didn't expect nor accept the responsibility of a new child.

That was the welcome that Taunton Scudder (without a documented father, he had been given his mother's maiden name) received on the rainy morning of his first breath. Local farmers who'd tried to grow crops in bad soil said that Taunton had sprouted from sour ground, and was destined to be a lollygagger. Years later, others less kind said that, "Taunton was born out of a whole family of boogers and that he'd did a fine job continuing the tradition." A year after his birth Taunton's mother married a distant relative, a person who shared her attraction towards substance abuse—a marriage that ensured Taunton would grow up in the same family atmosphere as his mother.

Taunton, or Taut as others came to call him—because he always seemed like a rope stretched too thin; psychologically ready to break at any moment—never met his dad, and wasn't close to any of his known relatives. (And it hadn't taken long for others to learn they'd better not call him belittling nicknames, at least to his face. That is unless a person wanted to be punched in the nose.) Neither his mother nor his mother's parents cared whether the boy lived or died. But his turbulence was more than physical, it was also emotional. Not only did the child feel neglected and abandoned by someone whom nature demanded that he trust, but that rejection was reinforced one day when his biological mother angrily announced, "You know that your birth wasn't planned! Just an accident you was, that's all just a bad accident."

This early-learned emotional disappointment sowed a seed fertilized by hatred that matured into a miserable being, one that some questioned would never reach mental maturity or ever be able to make rational decisions. But there was another side to Taunton, one that his critics didn't see. Perhaps the boy's faultfinders never got to really know him. Not only did he rage a tangible battle, but a psychological clash as well—conflict best described as the forces of good and evil fighting over who was going to win the boy's soul. We must remember that, after all, it takes two to have a child; that for every evil thing his mother was, his dad wasn't. Perhaps we shall see.

Taunton, the first name a great grandmother (his GG or also called Gram) had insisted on, came from her family's deep rooted respect of their historic birthplace of Taunton, England —a location from which pilgrims had embarked in 1639 when only to spend months cramped in the holds of little ships. Eventually the wayfarers touched land at a geographical place in the New World ultimately designated Massachusetts. The settlers had named the hamlet after their British home, a place that honored God, a truth especially important in middle of the 17th century when the wayfarers landed among the heathens of the new world.

The GG had suggested the first name of Taunton, praying the moniker would offset the terrible family name of Scudder. The Scudder clan in rural Maine had a reputation of socially abnormal behavior, and laziness, a dullness, at least when it came to honest work. *After all,* the great grandmother thought, *establishing a proper first name was the only practical thing to do.*

His Gram, who lived three miles from the Scudder family, provided the only positive female relationship Taunton could remember. She was an elderly, frail, grayed old lady who generally cared about the young boy. When seasons changed, she ensured that he had warm mittens, hat, coat and boots during cold weather, and for warmer days, she kept his shirts, pants and hats mended and patched.

GG often asked him to come to her small cottage to mow her lawn or shovel a walkway or some other errand that camouflaged her effort to provide him with warm, nutritious food and ensure he was properly dressed. Actually the great grandmother's attention had quite an effect on the youth's attitude towards others, and if she been able to live a few years longer, Taunton might have turned out differently. In fact Gram had wanted to adopt the pre-teen, but the mother said, "Of course you can have the boy—for only $10,000 *for the privilege.* On her meager social security the GG just didn't have that kind of money and so she remained content to help as often as she could in her humble (and very quiet) way.

Early on Taunton's grandmother had snuck the boy (because the mother would never have approved, so the elder knew better than ask) to the local church where the youngster sang along to the popular hymns of the time such as *I Come to the Garden Alone, How Great Thou Art,* and the Hank Williams classic *'I Saw the Light.'* Taut had an entertaining voice, and the congregation was pleased whenever he sang. GG made the effort to teach the boy and, for a while he seemed to respond, but then the gram got sick and the boy slipped away from Christian teachings.

Unfortunately his gram suffered an irreversible stroke when Taunton turned nine, and she was admitted to a nursing home where the boy's only psychological support spent her remaining days. The grandson never saw his gram again. After that, there was only one other woman who would have a positive effect on the boy, and he met her years after his great gram had passed. Unless pressed, Taunton might not admit it, but trusting a woman didn't come easy for him, a topic he wouldn't discuss.

But in today's adult world, the man Taunton had few friends, little money, and he wasn't sure if there even was a God. On too many Sunday mornings while nursing a hangover he'd heard television evangelists instruct tithing because 'the electronic flock didn't need to save for sickness, children's college, or retirement. Living room parishioners only needed to mail in *seed money* to the television address and *god would return ten-fold. Giving hard earned money away just didn't make no sense,* he rationalized—*nope, just not practical.* Not that his income was ever hard-earned. He'd always lied, cheated, or stolen to get whatever he wanted. *Hey, that was just his heritage and the practical thing to do.*

Actually his independence had started years before, when in the middle of seventh grade Taut decided he had enough of discipline and living up to the expectations of others, so the juvenile had run away. Oddly his transition to independence occurred the same year his mother and step-father divorced.

Those that knew Taut said the handsome boy wore 'nice' whenever he chose, but seemingly beyond the boy's control, Scudder's appearance would suddenly change. A charming smile could abruptly turn into a snarl as his eyes turned glassy and his face contorted, like an unseen force had taken hold. Then just as quickly, the black cloud that covered his face would drift away and the boy's charm would return; it was a tool he'd use to get what he wanted. Girls, booze, even jobs, came his way, but none lasted long. Taunt, too lazy to be tied down, never stayed bound to anyone or anything very long. According to 'them-that-know,' who visited the coffee shop every morning, the boy hadn't learned to be lazy, he'd been born that way."

Then one night Taunton met Margaret Woodward's mother, Pauline. He'd been watching the widow ever since he'd read the husband's obituary in the newspaper. Always looking for opportunity, he viewed now-single-parent-Polly as someone who was a free ticket to gambling, carousing and visiting dark places that some only whispered about. Pauline, lonely and needing the income a husband could bring, quickly became infatuated by the handsome, charming man. She never saw a sign of the hatred or the irritability that was to come.

Once he'd joined her wedding bed, Polly discovered the turbulent life she had married into, one completely different than the previous relationship which had created a beautiful, loving daughter. The new Mrs. Scudder did whatever was necessary to ensure that her only child, Margaret Woodward, a surname kept from the previous marriage, was safe. But Taut hated the relationship Margaret had with her mother. He nicknamed the girl 'Miss Maggie Magoo,' to make it clear to both who was the boss. He'd see to it that the 'ridiculous closeness of the mother/daughter relationship would come to an end. *No-sir-ree, there wasn't a woman alive who could be trusted,* he had justified, *just wasn't practical to believe any of em.*

•••••••

Taut had read about his Miss Magoo's literary award in the Penobscot Basin Times and figured she needed help managing all that money. Standing in the shadow of an alleyway, out of the heat of the day of Jim's remembrance, he guzzled a cold beer to offset the increasing humidity while he watched and waited. Once Margaret had passed inside the church he lit a smoke and grinned at the opportunity for a reunion with his now favorite step-daughter. *After all Maggie was family, wasn't she!* He'd coldly grinned.

Before Taut knew it, the people were exiting the church. Some were getting into their cars and driving home, only to return moments later with their pot luck contributions. Others were heading towards wooden tables, barbeque grills and coolers, all set in place for an afternoon picnic. While two men laid kindling in a fire ring, others broke out instruments such as guitars and fiddles to demonstrate respect and celebrate the life of a friend.

Sucking up his fourth beer, Taunton saw Margaret depart the church, walking beside an older woman with a golden retriever at her side. He sneered and wondered who the black-headed woman could be? She looked kinda familiar, as if perhaps he had met her once. When the dog stared in his direction and growled, Taunton Scudder faded deeper into the shadows and turned to go about his 'practical business.'

THE RANGER'S WIFE
THE JIM CLARK SAGA
CHAPTER 9

A Child Is Born

Today Dr. Higgins scolded, "Young lady you just ruined my bird hunting trip!"

— Susan's Diary, October 26th

After the day of remembrance, Susan sat alone in her living room reading excerpts about Jim's and her time together, such as the time when the couple first learned that she was pregnant.

Susan hadn't felt well for some time. Her stomach had been upset and it had been hard for the 34-year-old woman to keep her food down. By the end of June, Jim had insisted that she travel the 70 miles to her doctor to find out what was wrong. Susan hadn't wanted to go. *Surely it's just a passing bug or perhaps she had drunk some bad spring water,* the wife had explained. Susan enjoyed their Umsaskis Lake home, and the couple had recently received news that they were next in line to adopt a child. So, Susan was sure there was nothing to worry about.

In their various assignments the couple had enjoyed the

children of the neighborhoods and had decided to have an infant of their own. But after a couple of years of trying, with no success, the couple was told that neither could have children. So they decided to adopt.

For two years the husband and wife traveled from their woods abode to the adoption agency in Waterville to receive training in the care and responsibility of raising a child. The couple would take a four-wheel Ranger pick-up to their personal car stored in Millinocket, then after the three hour-trip to town, they would drive an additional three hours for their training. The distance required an overnight stay, after which they would rise early the next day, resupply and then return to their log home.

That winter the agency had even told the couple that they would send a caseworker to live with them for several days, to ensure that 'theirs was a proper home in which to raise a child. One February Jim had met the agent in Millinocket, and driven him in the all-wheel-drive truck over narrow icy roads 100 miles to the driveway of 'the lodge.' It had been a harrowing ride for the emissary from Waterville. After sliding down the road a couple of times to avoid hitting a moose, and dodging three loaded logging trucks on their way to the Great Northern Paper Company mill in Millinocket, the two men had arrived within a mile of the couple's wilderness cabin. But the driveway wasn't plowed, so they left the comfort of a warm truck and slipped into cold weather suits and helmets to make the last leg of the trip by snowmobile to Susan, waiting at the camp.

Jim and Susan had thought the visit with the caseworker had been ok, and then their feelings had been confirmed, when in April they'd received a letter from the Waterville 'Home for Little Wanderers' confirming approval of their application.

Then the following June, they received a certified letter that said they were next on the list to receive a child, and could expect to come to Waterville by early summer to pick up their infant. Excitedly, the husband and wife began gathering the clothes, toys, bottles, diapers and other supplies necessary for a newborn. "And yes, Jim," Susan had replied to her husband's inquiry, "I do think it is too early to buy the little one a hunting rifle!"

Just when things were looking up, Susan started feeling down.

The drinking water for the ranger's camp lay 200 feet uphill from the cabin. The spring water, stored in a covered concrete reservoir, stayed clear and cool in a tank which had been established at a high elevation above camp so gravity pulled the water directly into the building, thus eliminating the need to run generators and water pumps to supply sinks and showers. For over a year the couple had drunk the water, and thought it was the best tasting spring water in the North Woods. But now that the woman's stomach ached, and Jim was concerned that the spring had become contaminated by a dead squirrel, frog or algae; and although he had checked the cement basin, he hadn't found anything wrong. Just to make sure, Jim had even poured a half-gallon of bleach into the tank, and flushed it through the black plastic water line, to kill any bacteria that may be lurking about unseen. Even after all of that, Susan's stomach still hurt and she was feeling funny...not hungry...sensing something was wrong, Jim insisted they drive to her physician at the Presque Isle Hospital.

In the examination room, after giving the woman a physical, Doctor Higgins had pointed at the lady's stomach and said "what do you think that is?" Susan had known her stomach was getting bigger, and she had prayed it wasn't a tumor. She could never break that news to her husband.

"I don't know!" Susan had said, nervous about what the prognosis might be.

"You're five months pregnant."

The unbelievable had happened! She couldn't wait to tell

Jim they were going to have their own child!

Once a month after that. Susan would return to Presque Isle for a routine checkup and all was progressing as expected. The doctor even made plans for the delivery. "You know Susan," Doc Higgins had laughingly said. "I have my pilot's license and my plane is on floats. When the time comes, I can fly in, make the delivery and just to ensure everything is ok, I'll hang around a few days."

"But Doctor Higgins, I can't ask you to just wait for me to recover from the birth."

"Don't think anything of it. I love to hunt and fish." He'd smiled in anticipation of a vacation on the lake.

Now Susan understood the Doctor's real reason why he offered the personal attention.

But on October 20th Susan's blood pressure had risen too high too quickly. So it was best that she be admitted into the hospital. The night of her first bed check, Doctor Higgins had announced, "Young lady, you just ruined my outing to the woods!" At 11pm, on October 26th, the couple welcomed a new daughter into the world.

But it was what had occurred the previous September that made the arrival of a child even more significant.

THE RANGER'S WIFE
THE JIM CLARK SAGA
CHAPTER 10

Inferno

Someone was pounding on our bedroom door hollering, "Get up! get up! There's been a fire!"

— Susan's Diary, September 12th

Then there was the stress of the fire…

I am not sure if it's worse to see my hubby go away from home or have him return, the woman thought after she had seen her ranger husband off on his weekly patrol route. He was expected to be gone for at least three days. It was always hectic when her spouse left. She had gotten up at the crack of dawn and rushed to make sure he had enough food, packed his rain gear, matches, sleeping bag, compass and axe, as well as anything else needed to survive in the elements. She confirmed that he had packed his flashlight, two-way radio and first aid kit, because a person just never knew when an emergency would come to call.

Living in the middle of the Maine woods is different. After a hectic morning in their year-old Churchill Depot cabin, Susan relaxed for a minute before she started her own routine as a secretary, and smiled to herself, knowing Jim would laugh if he'd learned of her thoughts.

Alone, she sits in his chair, a captain's seat at the head of the maple hardwood kitchen table, and waits for her tea to steep. She stares unseeing through their picture window at the lake. The only sounds heard in the woods camp are the soft hiss from the gas lights, the tea kettle announcing it's time to turn the propane stove off, and the day's weather forecast emitting from the state's two-way radio. Their third golden retriever, Misty, lolls by her feet, lying with one paw on the woman's sneaker so the dog will know immediately if the female moves.

From nearby Heron Lake, a swimming loon offers its own weather prediction, and outside the kitchen window, the lady of the house hears the beating of hummingbird wings. The little creature's wings thump and thrash so fast they are barely visible. A half a dozen of the little birds dart in the air and argue about who will have the first sip of the red sugar water waiting in the feeder.

Susan's mind drifts back to how she came to live in the North Woods and reflects about her life in Maine's northern forest...

The young couple was excited, they were going home. Not home in the sense of returning to a place of residence, but back to the woods. Both Jim and Susan had grown up hiking and canoeing around the wilds of Baxter State Park. Leaving Cobscook Bay State Park and their friends and extended family behind, they smiled as they drove by Mt. Katahdin on their way to a new home: the   supervisor's lodge for the Allagash Wilderness Waterway on Umsaskis Lake.

The lodge, former VIP accommodations for International

Paper Company, and subsequently used by Maine's Department of Conservation when the waterway was established in 1966, would have been at home on the slopes of a Colorado mountain or in the wilds of Alaska. But for years the 'lodge' and its occupants had experienced a bedlam of troubles.

When Jim had received his promotion to the supervisor's position, the department's director had alluded to problems the agency was experiencing in the woods *and that Jim was to catch and deal with the prankster.* The couple arrived at the headquarters and immediately began receiving information about acts of vandalism occurring throughout the watershed. Repeated reports of break-ins to both state and private property had occurred at an alarming rate. There wasn't any structure, vehicle, or equipment that was exempt from sabotage. Sinks were broken off walls, mattresses stood up against walls and blasted full of holes by a shotgun. Personnel files were removed from the park office, gas lines cut, water added to gas tanks, windows broken, holes chopped in canoes, and guns and cameras locked securely inside buildings suddenly turned up missing. Whoever was doing it apparently didn't want others trapping in the area. Trappers checking their sets often found their traps sprung, and more than once a trapper would return to his one-room cabin only to find that someone had soaked the inside of the building with gasoline. The waterway's headquarters wasn't exempt from these acts.

Just as Jim was beginning to get an idea on who was doing the vandalism, he and Susan received an invitation to a surprise baby shower to be held for the couple at Reid State Park in Georgetown.

Leaving the yard, Susan and Jim wondered what they would find on their return. Would a gas line be cut, tires flattened on their 4x4, water hose left running so their spring water would be dry, or would the new electric line running from the generator house to the cabin be sliced?

The day at the baby shower was pleasant, with dozens in attendance congratulating Jim and Susan and showering them with gifts for the child-on-the-way. Then at midnight the couple was awakened with a call saying their home had been lost. Jim kissed his wife good-by and headed to Umsaskis to survey the damage.

Three years later the couple and their daughter moved into a new headquarters at Churchill Dam where Susan now enjoyed her morning or early afternoon, or evening tea.

THE RANGER'S WIFE
THE JIM CLARK SAGA
CHAPTER II

A Midnight Caller

1:30 this morning a truck drove into our yard without headlights ... — Susan's Diary March 3rd

It wasn't unusual for her husband to be gone all day. Susan completely understood if Jim came home late, or if an emergency had occurred; causing him to be gone overnight, or even longer. Susan knew that her husband would call her through the state's two-way radio communications to advise if he had been delayed and when he'd be home. The woods-woman wasn't worried. It was winter and the State hadn't yet constructed a replacement headquarters, so the couple had bought a small camp off the Turkey Tail Road along an area known as Partridge Cove on the shore of South Twin Lake; a location a few miles off route 11 south of the Hamlet of Millinocket. Susan stayed at their home when Jim needed to travel into the Allagash.

Then, well after midnight, while their 3-year-old daughter

slept upstairs in her crib, Susan heard the sound of a vehicle entering their driveway without its headlights turned on. Still recovering from the loss of their Umsaskis home and completely knowledgeable about the vandalism still occurring, Jim had insisted that she keep a loaded .38 caliber Smith & Wesson revolver, out of reach of their child, but close by never-the-less.

Using the light from the moon shining through the bedroom window, Susan arose from bed without flipping on the light switch, slipped on her housecoat, and reached for the holstered revolver from the top shelf in the bedroom closet. Unsheathing the Ruger Speed-Six stainless-steel handgun, she checked to see if the firearm's cylinder was loaded with shells. Confirming the ammunition she grasped the firearm firmly in her right hand, and eased into the kitchen, moving cautiously so she could look through the glass window of the entry door—to see, but not be seen.

Outside in the cold night air, a dark-colored pickup stopped half-way up the driveway, and she heard the engine being silenced. When Susan saw a man exit the vehicle and quietly walk toward their cottage without a flashlight, she pulled back the hammer of the handgun and flicked on the outside flood lights. If the man tried to break in, he'd be sorry. *Her little girl would not be harmed!*

•••••••

It has been another long day, Jim thought as he strapped the snowmobile into the bed of his 4x4 half-ton truck. The ranger's day had started before dawn. His wife and child were still asleep when he'd quietly made a lunch to complement a thermos of hot-ice-tea and then had gone out to scrape the ice from the windshield of his patrol pick-up.

The previous evening he'd loaded the pick-up with his snowshoes, snowmobile suit, helmet, flashlight, emergency pack, field glasses, two-way portable radio, extra dry coat and other provisions needed to spend a day in the deep woods— ensuring he had everything necessary to return, even if it meant he experienced minor equipment failure. Late that night he'd tucked his kid in bed, and with a goodnight kiss reminded her that he wouldn't be there in the morning because he had an appointment at Churchill Dam. But he said he should return home to the T4 Indian Purchase TWP in time for supper.

During that time of morning when it isn't night and not yet day, Jim started the truck and idled the vehicle long enough to warm the engine, slightly but not long enough to wake his still sleeping family. Then the man left home in a cold blue dawn with, the eastern sun just breaking through the morning chill.

Jim's plan was to spend the day in the woods, meeting with rangers, fisherman, sporting camp operators, and landowner foresters to review harvesting plans. It was sure to be a day full of resolving issues, rescuing stranded visitors, training staff, enforcing regulations and interpreting the area's wild values.

By the time Jim had loaded the snowmobile back onto the 4x4, the vehicles dash clock displayed the time 8 o'clock. *Too late for supper again*, the ranger thought, leaving Chamberlain Bridge where he had parked the 4x4 for the day. Cold and hungry, Jim was anxious to hear what his family had been up to while he was working; and he was only 70 miles away. Opening a can of Vienna sausage and Ritz crackers, Jim snacked as he drove along the icy road.

The truck that Jim was driving had been a dependable 1978 four-wheel drive that had carried the ranger-supervisor safely home many times. But during the Umsaskis fire, the truck had been parked near the couple's bedroom. In the illuminating glow of the burning lodge, fire crews had arrived, and not having keys to the truck and seeing the vehicle close to burning along with the camp, the woodsmen had hooked a chain onto the automobile and dragged the 4x4 out of harm's way. But the truck didn't completely escape injury. The vehicle was sent to a repair shop at Lake Saint George State Park, where repairs were completed, fenders repainted, and the transportation put back on the road. Well almost all of the overhauls were found.

Heading home on the Telos Road after the long day on sled patrol, the truck's heater was doing its job. Relaxed and settled in for the now 60-mile drive home, Jim emptied his thermos of the last gulp of hot-ice-tea. But, when he reached the bottom of Harrington Lake Hill near the bridge over the West Branch of the Penobscot River, the ranger's mood suddenly changed.

Without warning, the headlights failed and the vehicle's heater fan stopped working. Pulling off to the side of the road, Jim found that not only were the headlights out, but so were the brake lights, marker lights and even the caution blinkers. With a flashlight Jim changed the vehicle's fuses, and immediately the overloaded circuits burnt in protest. The ranger supervisor didn't have a lot of options. [3]

At 9:30 at night, and -10°F, it was cold, and with the nearest camp 25 miles behind, Jim weighed his possibilities. It was too cold to try and run the engine until dawn, which wouldn't do any good anyway. Jim was about to unload his snow sled and return to Chamberlain Bridge and to the nearest camp, when drifting clouds exposed a brilliant full moon.

The natural glow was so powerful that Jim decided to continue the drive. *After all he was now only 35 miles from home, a warm bed and his family.* Two hours later; much to the amazement of a log truck and three pickups who met a ranger truck driving without headlights, Jim arrived at his South Twin Camp.

---

[3] Author's note: This story is a true representation of an experience that Tim Caverly had one winter during a night time drive to his camp on South Twin Lake. Later inspection of the 4x4 found that the truck's electrical wires, partially melted by the heat of the headquarters fire, had received further damage when the truck's movements chafed through the copper cord's insulation, which caused the electrical system to short circuit against the metal frame.

Once in his driveway, in order to not awaken his family, Jim parked halfway down the driveway and walked in the moonlight path towards the front door. Reaching to place his key into the door knob, he was surprised when the front door light snapped on.

Immediately the door opened, and with a relieved smile of welcome, Susan lowered the gun and eased the hammer of the six-shooter down into a non-firing position. With the weapon pointed towards the ground and away from the fully-relieved husband, the wife threw her left arm around her partner's neck and pulled him close.

Through the Crest of the Red Cardinal

A bulletin about the families of the northern forest

A little wartime drama at the Soper Mountain Watchman's camp with watchman Lawrence Deblois back in 1943

Woodsman
Sought in Maine
On Shooting

Greenville, Maine., Aug. 2nd (AP)

A bearded woodsman, sought for questioning about the mysterious slaying of Westley F. Porter of Patten, was believed trapped today between Eagle and Churchill Lakes, some 60 miles northwest of Webster Lake, where Porter was shot to death on June 3rd while guiding three Massachusetts fishermen. Posses called for additional manpower and bloodhounds.

The bloodhounds and Maine Police search team were to be flown from Greenville today to the remote and wild scene of one of Maine's biggest manhunts in recent years.

Ray O'Donald, a forestry plane pilot, brought word here yesterday that two members of the 40-man posse had escaped injury Saturday night when a shot was fired through the window of a cabin at Soper Mountain where they had stopped to rest. They were Bert Duty, a fish and game warden, and a forestry firewatcher named Duclois.

Soper Mountain is near Eagle Lake, where State Trooper James W. Mealey said he saw the armed woodsman on Friday. Mealey said the man was carrying a shotgun and a pack-basket and that his clothing was in tatters.

Porter, who was 46 and the father of 7 children, was slain with a shotgun.

Article courtesy of the Forest Fire Lookout Association of Maine

Authors Note: For more information about this manhunt, see Tim's book, *Wilderness Ranger's Journal*

THE RANGER'S WIFE
THE JIM CLARK SAGA
CHAPTER 12

Hermon LeBlanc

Then there was the most unusual employee...

...This morning an assistant ranger arrived an hour late to work. When the young man got out of his car, Jim was surprised to see the man's face covered with little square imprints...

— Susan's Diary, September 1st

Well, this certainly has been an interesting summer. Sometimes I am not sure how Jim keeps up with it all, and today was another example. Last August, we had an assistant ranger request a transfer from the Umsaskis Lake District to a central Maine park so he could be closer to family.

When Jim tried to fill the position, he received instructions from the Department's Augusta office that an oceanside assistant ranger had advised the director he wanted to transfer into the Allagash. When Jim tried to question if the candidate was capable of handling the rigors of wilderness responsibilities, the bureaucratic boss stated that the Waterway wasn't any different than what was found at developed southern Maine parks. Therefore any assistant ranger in the system could fill any vacancy, regardless if they'd never handled a canoe and motor on a wild river.

So along came Hermon LeBlanc. He was a handsome spit-and-polish kind of guy who talked a good tale. But we soon learned his actions did not match his boasts. It didn't take long for the complaints to start rolling in. Other employees complained that Herman had little knowledge or experience with everyday field operations. Broken and lost equipment, outboard motor and chainsaw failures, neglecting to show up for work on time and getting lost, all combined to take district rangers time away from their responsibilities. Staff spent more time getting Herman out of jams, than conducting resource protection and public safety responsibilities.

Then Herman was assigned to help to clear the Priestly Mountain hiking trail to the old forestry lookout tower. Partway up the climb, LeBlanc stopped to get a drink of water from nearby Drake Brook. The ranger continued to clear the trail with bush clippers and left instructions for Herman to catch up. Finally three quarters of a mile later the helper caught up to his ranger. The boss turned and asked, "Where's the ax? I need to cut this fir blow down!" Of course Herman had left the ax in the stream, three quarters of a mile behind.

Complaint after complaint flowed into Jim's office. Protests included that Herman begged for food at campsites, criticized guides in front of clients; wasn't completing his assignments, and exhibited rude behavior. Some even suspected he was responsible for missing cameras and field glasses. Then came the day when Herman filed his accident report.

He'd canoed to Long Lake Dam campsite to clean the tent ground. Now, folks need to understand that at that time rangers carried bulky ten-watt two-way radios for emergency communications. Those handsets weighed about ten pounds and were equipped with 20-inch-long wire-transmitting and receiving antennas. The top of each antenna was covered by a red plastic cap so if someone stubbed and fell, they wouldn't stab themselves in an eye.

Hermon, to anyone's knowledge, was the first person to ever trip over a tree root and drive a radio aerial up his nose. Impaled, he removed the antenna, and following the wire antenna came a stream of frothy red fluid. Paddlers who met Hermon canoeing back to camp were shocked when they saw a ranger motoring up the lake with a handkerchief stuck in his nose, the cloth ends of which dripped blood.

When that same day a respected guide complained that Hermon had tried to pick up his female sports by enticing his lady clients to visit his camp for wine, it was time to send Hermon back to southern Maine.

That night Jim radioed Hermon to let him know that he needed to meet with the assistant ranger the following morning at eight o'clock; to discuss employment. Jim arrived at camp at quarter to eight the following day, but there wasn't any Hermon to be found.

At 8:15 a.m. there wasn't any Hermon in sight, and at 8:30 still no assistant ranger. Jim was about ready to organize a search, when Hermon drove into the yard at a high rate of speed. When he jumped out of his car, red- faced and worried from being late, Jim saw Hermon's face crisscrossed with red checkerboard-type marks. The following is the direct explanation that Hermon offered about the marks on his face.

"Well, Jim, I knew that my work here had not gone very well. And when my friend Dale showed up last night, I told him that you were probably going to send me home. So he suggested that we should have a final night out at a nightclub across the border in Daaquam, Quebec."

Jim replied, "I'm listening," so Hermon continued.

"I think the bar was called *Pub Le Quartre par Deux*. Walking inside, we were immediately greeted by a middle- aged lady who welcomed us in French. Rock and roll music was playing, the crowd was laughing, and circling through the patrons was an assortment of pretty girls offering gents a dance for a dollar."

"Well, we had a few beers, which led to a harder mixture of rum and soda. Before I knew it, we were joined by other Americans who bought drinks and I began flirting with the girls. Well, trying to give one a compliment in French, apparently I said the wrong thing and the next thing I knew she'd slapped my face. Immediately a bouncer said it was time to leave; as I turned to go I tripped over a chair, and fell across a table, breaking the furniture."

"Dale grabbed my arm, and walked me to the seat on the passenger's side of his truck. Once back on the road, I kept falling asleep from the imbibing which caused me to slump over and lay my head on the driver's shoulder. Well, even though we are friends, he wasn't having any of that, so Dale put a fishnet over my head and tied the cord to the gun rack fixed over his back widow. I woke up this morning, still tied to the gun rack with the fish net over my head. When I realized the time, I rushed back and arrived here before the marks had time to disappear."

Obviously the man was embarrassed, so my husband simply told Hermon about his concerns for the assistant ranger's safety; now that fall had arrived, it was time for Hermon to return to southern Maine.

After Hermon left, Jim checked the building to make sure all was secure. Looking around the woodshed, he found four frozen moose legs. He remembered that earlier that summer he'd heard a report about a dead moose floating in the Long Lake thoroughfare. Soon Jim realized that Hermon must have cut off the front and hind legs most likely to use as the base for a lampshade. Jim understood that possessing parts of a moose without a license to hunt moose was highly illegal. So he threw three of the legs into the deep woods, but before he threw the fourth, the thought came to Jim that, *maybe I can do something with this.*

So, he tucked it under the front seat of his pickup and headed back to Churchill Dam. Almost back to the Dam, the leg started to thaw and emanated the smell of rancid meat. Jim pulled off beside the road to dispose of the rotted carcass and realized he was close to a marten trap that belonged to his friend Matt.

Walking into the forest, but not interested in tampering with the trap, Jim walked around the entrapping scene and stuck the leg into the mud about 20 inches directly behind the trap. An hour after returning to his headquarters, Matt drove into the yard and hollered, "Hey, Jim, I am going to check my traps, wanna go?"

"Sure," Jim replied. Within a few minutes they arrived at the trapping area Jim had visited earlier. Matt got out of his truck, looked low under the branches at his set and with astonishment turned to Jim and said, "There is a moose leg in my trap." Jim gave the only reasonable answer there could be. "I've heard that if a moose gets caught in a trap, he'll chew his leg off to get out."

It wasn't until years later that Jim finally told Matt about how the hooved leg got placed in the mud near the trap set.

THE RANGER'S WIFE
THE JIM CLARK SAGA
CHAPTER 13

Ouch!

Last night was very long and I felt bad for the young man in the stretcher...

— Susan's Diary, June 30th

Susan was preparing supper in the kitchen of their Churchill Dam camp, when she heard a loud pounding on the cabin's front door. Alone, because her husband Jim had gone to review cutting plans with a local forester and wasn't expected home for some time, she answered the door.

She was surprised to see a middle-aged man in a Boy Scout uniform. Out of breath, he announced, "One of my scouts has had an accident in Chase Rapids." Gasping for breath, he continued, "One of the canoes capsized and the boy who was in the bow is in the water and pinned between the canoe and a rock. I've radioed my Scout base and they have advised to leave the boy in the river. The base is flying our medical team with a stretcher in from the Scout base; we'll rescue him when they get here. But," the leader admitted and acting like he wasn't sure what to do next so he said, "the boy is awful cold. The force of the water is so strong that we can't move him or the canoe."

Susan had helped with similar incidents, and she knew immediately what to do. Grabbing the camps two-way radio, she contacted the nearest ranger at Camp Pleasant.

"Churchill Dam to 1704."

Immediately Ranger Pat replied, "Go ahead."

"We have a situation in Chase Rapids. A canoe has capsized and a boy is in the water pinned between his canoe and a rock just above the Devil's Elbow. "

"I am at the Jaws Campsite on Churchill Lake and will head down immediately. My ETA is 10 minutes. How many involved?" the ranger replied.

"One of the troop leaders is here with me now, and he says only one of his group of 12 is injured. The others are on shore and out of danger." Susan answered. "The hurt boy is in the river and there is a concern that he has a back injury."

Ranger Pat instructed, "We'll need to ease the pressure of the water flow to the rapids. There is a stretcher in the barn. I'll be right along to close the gates of the dam."

"10-4" (ok) Susan answered and offered, "I'll use the power wrench[4] and close the gates of the dam to relieve water flow to the river so the victim can be lifted off without further injury. That way you can continue with your emergency gear and head directly down the Portage Trail to the Elbow."

"10-4," replied Pat. "Almost at the Dam now. Have the leader take the stretcher towards the trail and I'll catch up to him."

---

[4] Authors note: The power wrench is a specialty chainsaw like tool that during the days of the wooden impoundment was used to open and close gates of Churchill Dam. The socket for the wrench cost $300 and the chain-saw type motor was so loud that rangers wore hearing protectors whenever using it.

"I'll remain at the dam to maintain emergency communications in case you need additional help." Susan offered.

"10-4" was the only reply.

Susan immediately instructed the troop leader, "Let's go. Night is approaching and we need to get the boy to safety." Acting much relieved, the leader admitted, "This is my first trip down Chase, and I guess I should have been better prepared."

Without commenting about the man's worry, Susan instructed, "Follow me." And with that she led the way to the Churchill supply barn. Inside she pointed out a light-weight stretcher to the leader and asked him to take the litter to the scene of the rescue. Although the weight of the power wrench made her groan, she was able to lug the wrench onto the Dam's walkway to close three of the impoundment's shallow gates.

Wearing the hearing protectors, the lady of the woods looked up in time to see the ranger's canoe pull up to the dock. Making distant eye contact, Pat waved to Susan to acknowledge he was on the scene, and immediately grabbed his rescue pack, hiked by the boarding house, and with purpose, hit the trail to the Big Eddy and the accident location which Pat knew to have a reputation for heavy white water.

Once the gates were shut, the C-F-S of the water flow in the river immediately lowered. Back at camp, 45 minutes later, she received a radio call from Pat, who advised, "The boy is stabilized on a stretcher and the rescue team is lugging the injured party back up the [mile-long] trail to the ranger's camp.

Pat further advised, "The victim was in the water for over an hour. His face is blue from the cold so he is suffering from severe hypothermia, and is complaining of lower back pain." We'll need warm blankets and a warm drink to return his core temperature to normal."

"10-4," Susan replied and then advised. "I've heard from the Scout base that they have a float plane on the way, but I am unsure if they will arrive before dark."

Pat replied, "Ok, if the aircraft arrives late, the boy may have to stay in the Churchill ranger's camp overnight."

With the news that the boy was in safe hands, Susan began making coffee, warming soup and making sandwiches because she expected the whole group would be cold and hungry.

Twenty-five minutes later, a float plane landed at the dock. Fifteen minutes after the arrival of the plane, by the time the rescue group had arrived at the ranger's camp, complete darkness had set in. When Susan heard footsteps on her porch, she opened the door and welcomed the rescued group to a previously warmed camp, the room illuminated by propane lights and she had hot refreshments waiting.

The injured boy was carried into the camp's living room, gently removed his wet clothing and wrapped him with blankets which had been warmed by the wood stove. EMTs from the plane treated the injured paddler.

In an hour and a half, and after Jim had returned, the scouts left to set up their tents at the Churchill Dam campsite, and Ranger Pat returned to his camp on Churchill Lake. Even though the boy had been stabilized, Susan was fearful for him, so she slept in her recliner that night. Whenever she heard the boy in the stretcher groan, she'd awake and recover him with the blankets that he had kicked off during a fitful sleep.

The next morning at dawn, the boy was carried to the plane and flown to the Arthur Dean Hospital in Greenville. Susan, along with the rest of the troop, stood on the dock and thankfully wished the boy well on his flight towards recovery.

THE RANGER'S WIFE
THE JIM CLARK SAGA
CHAPTER 14

Are the Antics Worth the Pain?

Today Jim returned home with an old wooden spoke wagon wheel in the back of his truck...

– Susan's Diary, July 10th

Taunton Scudder left the funeral-style memorial service and returned to his pick-up parked nearby. Nearing the 4x4, Taunton viewed it as run-of-the-mill — that was how the man had planned it. When he drove his Dodge Ram out and about 'tending to practical business,' ole Taut didn't need anything that would stick out. In fact, his truck could be best described as dusty neutral tone in color, with wooden canoe racks, and windows so muddy, it would be hard to tell who might be inside. Headlights were kept clean so he could see moose at night, but everything else was common place for a woods vehicle. That was the way he kept it. He'd even gone so far as to spray oil onto the vehicle's license plates, and rubbed them with mud so the truck's registration number couldn't be identified. His truck looked the same as a hundred others that might be seen on any given day in the middle of the Maine woods.

After two hours, he entered through the Telos Checkpoint on his way deeper into the North Woods. Driving by the ranger station at Chamberlain, Taunton thought about inventorying the park's workshop, but also understood there might be a trail camera somewhere watching the tempting prize. Through experience he'd learned someone could drive by at any minute, so Taunton decided to check facilities deeper in the woods.

Finally arriving at Churchill Dam, he saw there were several parties waiting to have their gear portaged around Chase Rapids. Killing time for the people to clear, he parked in front of the old storage barn and walked through the open door of the park's small museum. Inside was a map of the village when it was a logging depot with so many pet dogs that the French had slanged their home, "Ville dé Chien." There was a child's desk from one of the two schools that once served the lumbermen's families of Churchill Village. Two schools, one that taught English and the other which instructed in French, served the community so both cultures could ensure their values would remain intact.

Centered in the room was a brightly-painted rebuilt horse-drawn-belly-dump gravel wagon, a conveyance used around 1905 to build Long Lake Dam. Years before, the wagon had been discarded after the water impoundment had been completed. For years the wood had rotted and metal parts had rusted and laid waste, until 1995 when a husband and wife volunteered to recover and transport the corroded parts by a canoe, and then spent 300 hours restoring the wagon to new condition.

Though the project was estimated to cost $7,000, volunteers tolled and got the job done by spending only $1,800 for materials.

Taunton stared at the wagon and remembered years before, when one of the wheels had served as a chandelier in the now-burnt Page Camp — a wheel, he'd almost taken home. The log cottage had been located due east from the Grey Brook campsite on the south end of Long Lake, 5 ½ miles south of Long Lake Dam.

At the time, Taut had been offered several hundred dollars if he could steal the wheel, so he watched and waited until the Umsaskis ranger was headed south toward the lake's inlet to make his move. Using a 20-foot Grumman with an 8 horse Mercury outboard, Taunton made the trip to the camp from the Umsaskis parking lot.

It wouldn't take long and he was sure he'd be back with the wheel long before the ranger returned from his patrol. Arriving at the log cabin Taunton kicked the door open and once inside, dragged the camp's kitchen table under the light. Standing on the table, he used an adjustable wrench to first undo one of the bolts of the four boom chains that secured the heavy chandelier light to the building's log rafter. But Taunton underestimated the weight of the wooden wheel and so when he removed the bolt to the second chain, the heavy wheel swung down like a pendulum. When he tried to catch it, the combined weight of him holding the wheel broke the table and Taunton fell backwards landing on the floor across an over-turned chair.

Taunton thought he'd broken his back, with an injury so bad that the pain was beyond belief, he crawled to the canoe. After a few pulls of the outboard, he was able to get it started and motored back to the bridge at the Reality Road. In agony, there wasn't any way he could load his canoe onto the truck, so Taunton hid the craft in the woods and limped his way back to the vehicle with plans to get his canoe after a couple of days' rest. If anyone had seen Scudder limping slowly under torture, they would have thought he'd been in a bad car accident.

Taunton learned that several days later, Jim Clark, while on patrol, had found the Page Camp broken into and the wheel chandelier hanging by two chains. Jim had been afraid whoever had tried to steal it would return, so he had enlisted the aid of one of his rangers and taken the wheel to Churchill for safekeeping. There the artifact had remained under lock and key until years later when it was needed to restore the historic wagon.[5]

On damp days Taunton could still feel the weakness in his back caused by the run-a-way wheel. Returning to the task at hand, Taunton stood in the barn, and looked through a crack in the old door at the canoe landing on the west side of the river. Once he determined it was all clear, and that everyone had left the area, he could now finish his business.[6]

Walking to the west shore behind the boarding house, where the watercourse narrowed, Taunton waded two feet into the river and removed a rope tied to an underwater piece of discarded steel boom chain. He then strolled back across the dam, with day pack in hand, and when he neared the big pine close to the ranger station, he decided to knock on the door of the ranger's camp to see if anyone was watching. When he didn't receive an answer, Taunton tried the door and was pleased to find it unlocked. Careful not to leave any dirty footprints on the floor, he looked about the cabin. Hanging off a wall-mounted gun rack was a rifle, a Remington 30-06 with a scope. Since it wouldn't do to be seen coming out of the cabin

---

[5] Author's note: The rebuilding of the antique wagon is an accurate account of the reconstruction by a couple who wishes to remain anonymous.

[6] Author's note: The incident of a vandal's efforts to steal the wagon wheel did occur. The wheel served as a light fixture in the former Page Camp on Long Lake, and there was an attempt to steal it as described above, The relic was recovered by Supervisor Tim Caverly before the spoke wheel could be illegally removed. While rangers never learned who tried to pilfer the artifact, that wheel remains today, safely bolted in place on the right rear of the restored wagon, resting secure in the old LaCroix Supply Barn at Churchill Dam.

carrying another's firearm, Taunton picked up the edge of the living room's fold-out couch, laid the weapon underneath, and placed the cushions back in place. *With any luck, the ranger would think it was stolen and never look for it to be hidden in the state camp.* Taunton could then return at a quieter time, perhaps even hunting season, break into camp and claim his prize.

Once that little project was completed, without leaving any evidence behind, he strolled to the bank of the river and waded again into the water. There he untied the other end of the ½-inch strand and pulled the line in. Once he had the rope on shore, he was pleased to see that there were over 3-dozen assorted fishing lures—rapala's, mooselook wobblers, along with dardevles and a good number of trout flies. A few years back Taunton learned that by securing a heavy line in such a manner underneath the water, well out of sight, fishermen would hook their lures into the rope. Figuring they had snagged a sunken log, the sportsmen would break the monofilament line leaving their lures behind. *Most of 'em looked to be in good shape,* Taunton thought as he remembered the black market where he could sell any amount of fishing equipment that normally brought him enough money for beer and cigs. *After all, it was the practical thing to do.* With that, Taunton curled the rope with lures attached to remove at his leisure, saving the braided line to reset another day.

It was time to set up his tent, gather firewood for supper and then he could get a good start early the next morning to see if the pig's-head was doing its job.

Through the Crest of the Red Cardinal
A bulletin about the families of the northern forest

Allagash Wilderness Waterway Log Cabin Hit by Vandals
Unknown Assailants Cause Extensive Damage

Article complements of my good friend — author, and historian
Faye O'Leary Hafford

Maine Ranger's Investigate Vandalism
T16R11 WELS, Maine
October 1974

as transcribed by Park Receptionist
Faye O'Leary Hafford

Tonight my husband and I are feeling sad. We returned to camp the day after Halloween to find that some half-crazed individuals had broken into our cabin. A destruction which can only be explained as some sort of vendetta; the vandals

---

completely ravished our beautiful log cabin. Using axes, the hooligans smashed stoves, refrigerator, and bathroom facilities.

They cut doors off the cupboards, and smashed dishes. The office desk was overturned, and the door of the safe was ripped apart. Fortunately there was only $10.00 in the safe at the time.

Outside the building, the outboard motors, water pump and lawn mowers were ruined. The ranger truck had been pushed over the hill and into the river. Hundreds of gallons of gasoline, along with other equipment were stolen. An attempt was also made to vandalize a grader that belongs to Mabec Lumber Company which was parked in the ranger's parking lot.

This was the first year of my ranger husband's assignment in the river district and we couldn't help but wonder if we were the intended victims of the 'goblin trick.' We never did find out who the ruffians were, but one thing is certain, it was not a Halloween prank. Either this was an act of some psychopaths who were spaced out on drugs and alcohol, or it was an act of revenge for something that displeased the vandals. I believe the criminal act was a combination of both.

Author's Note: This incident is from a book by Faye O'Leary Hafford titled *Waterway Wanderings: A story of the people in the Allagash Wilderness Waterway, published in 1986.* The report is of an episode that occurred at the Michaud Farm Ranger Station in October of 1974.

Dear Reader,

Please allow me to pause in my manuscript, for perhaps this is the proper place to talk about Taunton Scudder's dad.

While I will disclose the name of Mr. Scudder's biological father, I must request that his name not be shared. For at one time Robert Woodward was a respected member of a Maine community, active in youth organizations and some say, on his way to high political office. But that lifestyle almost didn't occur.

Thank you for understanding.

Tim Caverly

THE RANGER'S WIFE
THE JIM CLARK SAGA
CHAPTER 15

The Search Begins

Today I picked up our mail at the Clayton Lake Post Office and received the strangest package. — Susan's Diary, July 14th

In his senior year of high school, Robert was a handsome six-foot-three-inch-tall teenager with a winning smile, a boy so good-looking that school girls could only speak in low whispers whenever he neared. As a student, he excelled in track, basketball, baseball and gymnastics. He won awards on the school's debate team and played the lead role in the school's one-act play competition. When not in school, Robert could always be found afield: hiking, fishing, hunting, and otherwise enjoying Maine's outdoor world.

But even with all of his capabilities, the young man was best summed up as genuine; there wasn't a jealous bone or a hint of being conceited in any part of his athletic frame. The lad was liked by all who met him. As a Senior, his academic prowess was recognized when he was elected into the prestigious National Honor Society. Then, due to his scholastic aptitude, it was announced in the spring that Robert was to be granted a four-year scholarship to the University of Maine for conservation law. The boy was well on the way to becoming a Maine game warden, a park or forest ranger. But then he erred.

The mistake occurred one perfect June night after the Junior-Senior prom. The blunder was with a girl who had a reputation as a run-a-bout. She had been so charming, her perfume subsequently alluring; encouraged by a full moon that hypnotically floated on the edge of a dark horizon, the perfect music emanating from the radio all blended a romantic interlude into an impeccable recipe for an unplanned pregnancy.

Once Robert had received the news, he accepted his responsibility for the girl's condition. The boy told his parents he planned to ask the girl to marry him. But his socialite mom and dad thought otherwise. The Scudder family had such a bad reputation that Robert's dad was positive that his mistake would cloud their son's bright future. Shortly after the family learned of the coming child, Bob's father announced they were selling their home and moving. The senior would finish out his final year of high school halfway across the country. Late that spring the young expectant father concealed his psychological torment beneath a tranquil exterior.

Robert protested leaving his first love behind, but the father insisted that the boy was not to see or even talk to the girl. To further ensure that there wouldn't be any communication, the boy was immediately flown to a far-off town, with arrangements made for him to stay with a distant relative.

At the time, little did Robert know that his parents carried a secret of their own, one that perhaps caused his folks to overreact. Years before, Bob's dad had also been caught up in the charm of romance. He, too, had impregnated a girl out of wedlock, and had the firsthand experience of being the target of small town rumormongers who fancied it their obligation to inform their community of any illicit activity. Bob's dad had also been forced to give his child up for adoption, and the patriarch had sworn the orphanage to a strict code of silence and paid them a considerable amount to keep the origin of Bob's older sister hush-hush.

Robert's friends back home kept him apprised of the health of the Scudder girl, and when they wrote that in March she had borne a son, Bob cried. First the original sin, then being powerless to satisfy his parenting obligation, ripped through the fiber of Robert's psychological being. The biological father felt that life's turmoil had doubled-down in a perilous game of hopeless jeopardy.

Eventually Bob went to college where he studied resource management with a minor in philosophy. He was searching, but not sure for what. The thought of having a child who he couldn't speak with or see, haunted him. Then during one philosophy class, Bob made the discovery that gave him purpose. And that was the power of amulets and how they touched human life and values. He was amazed to learn about lucky charms and the effect they had on the human psyche, and the supernatural beliefs from cultures that spanned the globe, especially plentiful in all religions. If there was an evil, there was a talisman with magical properties to combat the wickedness. Good fortunes came in many forms of possessions such as four-leaf clovers, crucifixes, statues, gemstones, coins, and pendants. During class he learned it was common knowledge that 19th-century Native Americans often wore clothing called ghost shirts to protect them from the white man's bullets. The talisman Robert liked the best, and seemed to have significant historical significance for his purposes, was the Bloodstone. *Yes,* he had thought after studying the topic for many hours, *this will fit the bill just fine. Just hope I am not too late.* Now all he had to do was to find the money to pay for the valuable jewel.

The deep green and opaque ancient gem sprinkled with little red spots of iron oxide was the amulet that fit his needs, one that originated from a religious conviction. In research, Robert had read that the legend of the stone came directly from the cross. According to legend, as Jesus died, blood dripped from the crucified Christ onto Jasper stone at the bottom of the wooden Christian symbol. The body's plasma stained the rock, which today, if immersed in water, turns the color of Sun red. Bob also found that the bloodstone was sometimes called the martyr stone.

To determine if the stone is genuine, one only has to rub the jewel on porcelain and if blood-red scars appear—then the charm is genuine. The rock, also the birthstone for March, is magical with healing properties dating back to 5,000 B.C. It is a symbol of justice, which brings good luck, builds self-esteem, induces dreams, and drives away negative energy, fighting evil and jealousy. The gemstone also cures ailments involving blood disorders, strengthens heart, and improves circulation in a body's lymphatic system. Other ancient beliefs included that the talisman increased strength, made the wearer invisible, and that it was so powerful, the gem could control weather.

The summer after college, Robert was hired to work for an environmental firm; he was so well liked that Robert ultimately moved up through the ranks. Each time that he was promoted it was with the idea of correcting what Robert considered short term, harmful management decisions. However the desire to correct the worst personal mistake he ever made kept Bob climbing the professional ladder, until the time came when the next logical step was to pursue politics. After his college loans were paid, he put aside 10% of each paycheck for that time when he could catch up with his heartfelt obligation. Finally he saved the $1,300 to purchase the deep green, opaque with red spots of iron oxide, black onyx ring as his way to help a child that he expected never to meet.

Thirty years after his graduation from college Congressman, Woodward sent the following letter to his niece Susan Clark. *It was the practical thing to do.*

Dear Susan,

I am sorry that I have not kept in touch with you and the family but life has been very hectic and my home is too far away to return to Maine. I have always felt very close to you, and your parents. I am writing today to ask a _very important_ favor.

You may not have heard (because my parents didn't want anyone to know), but one starry night during my junior year of high school, I made a mistake that ended in a pregnancy. I expected to fulfill my obligation, but my dad wanted to keep it quiet and my parents, thinking they were making the best decision for my future, decided we should move. Knowing I left a child behind has troubled me ever since. I understand the reputation of the mother's family and appreciate they don't have much to offer. I fully expect they may have told Taunton that I was dead.

I am concerned how the child has fared, or if he is

even still alive. For years I have been searching for some way to help. I now have an idea of what can be done. So here is my request.

Enclosed is a letter of notarized introduction and a key to safety deposit box number 7 in the Millinocket branch of the Bangor Savings Bank. In that strongbox you will find $20,000 in cash and a small jewelry box. I would like you to find my son, and give him the money, minus any amount you need to cover expenses. Please insist he wear the gem. The ring is a talisman that philosophy dictates will help with any emotional issues he may have experienced from not having a proper father.

I've also included my inscribed Bible, it might help the boy understand that I really do care.

I would search myself, but I have to be out of the country for a while. Our government has asked that I assist with an overseas assignment, and it is one from which I may not return. I cannot leave without letting my son know I cherish my offspring. The mother's last name was Scudder and at one time they lived in Bangor.

When and if I return, I will be in touch to hear if you've been successful. Good luck and God bless.

Love,

Your Uncle Robert

As a young girl, the uncle, Susan's mother's youngest brother, had been her favorite relative and her best friend. Although ten years older than Susan, he had been at their house during every special occasion and even taught her the latest dance moves. Susan had been heartbroken when he suddenly left, and her parents refused to tell her why and to where he'd disappeared.

During her next trip to Millinocket, Susan stopped in the Bangor Savings Bank and, after checking identification, the teller guided Susan into the rectangular vault that held a bank of strongboxes including safe deposit box number 7.[7]

---

[7] Author's note: When Robert called the bank, he specifically reserved safety deposit box number 7.

During philosophy class he'd learned that Christian doctrine taught that the number seven is considered a most religious figure for several reasons. One reported belief is that Christ made seven utterances while on the cross. Knowing the biological mother's history, Robert thought his son probably needed all the help he could get.

THE RANGER'S WIFE
THE JIM CLARK SAGA
CHAPTER 16

The Day After the Service

This morning Margaret joined Bella and me for our talk. — Susan's Diary, May 23rd

Early the next morning after the remembrance ceremony, Margaret arrived at the address Susan Clark had written on a napkin and found a telephone pole from which a yellow-street sign advised:

Caution
Golden Retriever
Crossing

Margaret knew she had found the right address and contemplated, *I'm not sure what today's meeting will be about, I certainly need answers to at least four questions. Why was the urn empty? What is the story behind the strange note she'd seen inside, and where did she have to go back to? Even more important, is Jim still alive?*

Pulling into the hot-topped driveway, Margaret noticed the modest tan-colored home blended well with the evergreen forest that framed it. Landscaped for a pleasing eye, along the west side of the manicured lawn there were brown remnants of double-French purple lilacs that had completed their cycle of spring blossoms. Along the south side of the house were perennial flower gardens, species of plants that ensured there would be summer colors and nectar for bees and hummingbirds, even if the raised beds weren't tended every day. Along with sunflowers, crabapple trees and a variety of shrubs ensured that song birds and others were welcome to visit.

Before she could knock, Susan opened the door dressed in a light blue cotton blouse, dungarees, wearing wool socks and moccasins. Susan said "Come in, come in, you are just in time for tea. Bella is already here. We are glad you've come and expect you have some questions." Smiling, Margaret allowed herself to be guided through a living room decorated as if the building was a log cabin in a remote forest. Maggie entered the kitchen of the well-appointed ranch, and sat at a mahogany table while the steeped brew was poured. Turning down an offer of a blueberry muffin, Bella began the conversation, "I saw you open the urn…"

Taking a sip of the hot drink, and caught red-handed and feeling uncomfortable, Margaret replied, "I know I shouldn't have but…"

With a raised hand, Susan stopped her in mid-sentence with. "That's ok, Jim expected you would."

"What? Why, how would he have…?" Margaret stammered, unable to complete her question.

"My dad," Bella continued "understood that a good

reporter is, well, I don't want to call nosy, so perhaps inquisitive is a better word—that you would want to know what was inside the barrel urn. That way he could convince you that he hasn't gone, and encourage you to return to the Ice Caves on Allagash Lake. There is something you need to pick up. By the way, he likes your graffiti on the white birch."

For the next three hours, Margaret listened. Sure, she'd ask occasional questions to verify she understood, as any good reporter would do, but mostly the journalist listened.

By early afternoon Margaret had learned that Jim wasn't dead, but merely tying up loose ends. Susan planned to join him shortly at his woods camp. However, the reporter learned that Jim had been diagnosed with prostate cancer and he had received the final prognosis while Margaret was conducting her interviews.

The family first heard about Jim's cancer two years before. During a routine blood test the hospital lab reported Jim's prostate-specific antigen or PSA level of 5. A year later a second blood test showed a PSA reading of over 6. The doctor ordered a biopsy of the gland. Results then revealed that Jim did indeed have a malignancy; not an excessively large tumor, but two of twelve samples returned positive for the disease.

At first, Brewer's Lafayette Family Cancer Center had recommended hormone treatments supplemented by 8½ weeks of pinpoint radiation. For a while his PSA readings had diminished, and as the hormone shots wore off, the analyses had risen back to dangerous levels of stage 3 melanoma. Doctors recommended removal of the prostate and when Jim didn't agree, they suggested the implanting of radiation particles into the gland.

"And if that doesn't work, then we should conduct Chemotherapy treatments," the doctor advised, "and those cycles' intravenous infusions can last for weeks, followed by a period of rest and then, if necessary more cycles." There wasn't any guarantee that any of the procedures would work. "Extensive medical visits and hospital overnights might occur." If left untreated, the cancer would progress. It could take weeks, months or maybe a couple of years for the disease to devastate his body.

Margaret was told that Jim had talked it over with his household and, rather than put his family through the grief, expense and the demands of running him to the doctor visits—the old ranger should return to his cabin in the woods. Margaret also learned that at about the same time as their meeting, Jim had been given a natural remedy of a locally grown mushroom called Chaga. The fungus considered the 'King of Medicinal Mushrooms,' as was explained, is a parasitic growth that occurs on white birch trees that are older than 40 years. Used for years as a dark tea, the dependent mushroom reduces inflammation, provides anti-aging for skin, and normalizes cholesterol and blood pressure. Most importantly for Jim, it would provide holistic, and nutritional medicine in the man's fight against cancer.

After an extended period, Susan turned to Margaret and asked, "Are you ready to return to Allagash Lake as Jim suggested?" Without waiting for an answer, Susan continued, "I feel we should resolve this task as soon as possible."

Margaret pulled out her phone to check her calendar, and after comparing schedules, it was agreed they would return to the North Woods the following Monday, a whole seven days away. Ever curious, the reporter hated to wait a whole week to get to the bottom of the mystery, but that would give her enough time to pay overdue bills, and explain to her editor why she needed more time away from work.

"How long will we be gone?" Margaret inquired.

"When one travels into the woods, one never really knows how long one will be away. It should only be a couple of days." The ranger's wife decided not to mention the possible dangers.

"Can we climb Allagash Mountain while we're there? I am thinking about writing a new a book and would like to take a few pictures."

"Sure," said Susan, "and after the hike, we can drive around to the upper stream and visit the Ice Cave Campsite."

I wonder what I need to pick up? Did I leave something behind? Margaret pondered. She always considered herself very thorough whenever packing,

About that time Susan's son, George, arrived so the mother asked him to bring up the family trunk from the basement and set it on the living room rug in front of the couch. Seated and curious in their own right, Jim's family watched Margaret slowly and carefully open the huge trunk. After sorting through a variety of treasured family heirlooms found in any household, Margaret was surprised to see the last item waiting at the bottom. The beautiful golden oak mini-strong box had its contents protected by a brass padlock—a wooden vault designed to keep something very important, very secure. Bella offered that Margaret should take the small box back to her apartment so the reporter could examine the contents in private. Before Margaret left, Susan instructed that if her schedule allowed, they would leave first thing in the morning and that Margaret should bring enough spare clothing for two or three days, a spare pair of boots, and her rain coat. Susan indicated that her sons would have the truck loaded with canoe, food, tent and tarp for their trip.

That night after Bella and Margaret had left, Susan sipped slowly on a glass of red wine, looking forward to when she would be reunited with Jim. She suspected that he was well on the way to preparing camp for her arrival. She was going to miss her in-town home, but Susan knew that Isabella would care for the residence until it became necessary for Susan to give up life in the woods.

Thinking about living along the Allagash, Susan remembered

the first time she had met Taunton Scudder, and hoped this trip into the wilderness, would allow her to finally follow through on her uncle's wishes. The meeting with Scudder had occurred during Jim's last summer being employed as Waterway Supervisor, when he'd asked Susan to help with an emergency situation.

THE RANGER'S WIFE
THE JIM CLARK SAGA
CHAPTER 17

The Rescue

I found a man in the most unusual condition today... — Susan's Diary, June 29th

Early this afternoon I received a two-way radio communication from Jim.

Yesterday, my husband had received word that a male canoeist was missing on Round Pond in T13R12. Today, Jim and the Michaud Farm Ranger are assisting game wardens with the search and rescue. The canoe was found upside down near the east shore by the Tower Trail and it is feared the man might have drowned. The whole area is being examined and no one knows how long the search will last. The subject is reported to be very overweight and takes losartan to control high blood pressure.

Jim radioed to request that I fuel up the spare ranger truck and bring a two-way radio and extra supplies to Henderson Brook Bridge; just upstream from Round Pond. He instructed that I should radio him when I got close to the bridge, and he'd meet me at the landing.

It didn't take long to load the supplies. I packed extra radio batteries, bottled water, food, dry clothing, blankets, and mixed gas for outboard motors, as well as extra sleeping bags, spare canoe paddles, matches, thermoses of coffee, and sandwiches. In these instances, we never know how long a search will last.

Wouldn't you know I'd get a flat tire 10 miles from Henderson Brook Bridge and there wasn't any help in sight. I used the wagon jack to lift the truck, but the wheel's lug nuts were too rusted for me to budge. Fortunately outfitter Norman L'Italien of St. Francis came along. After he sprayed the lug nuts with WD-40 lubricant, we were able to change the tire so I could continue.

With a hearty thank you and my invitation for him to stop into our camp for coffee and pie, Norm waved and drove north as I steered the 4x4 southeast toward the river.

About three miles from Henderson Brook Bridge, I contacted Jim. He said that the crew was just completing a grid search, and he'd meet me at the crossing in about 45 minutes.

In the parking lot 500 feet from the bridge, I saw a dust covered pick-up with wooden canoe racks. At the gravel put-in, I found a 20-foot canoe beached on shore with a man sitting in the stern seat leaning back, passed out against the rear deck. Quickly I ran to see if I could help and was glad to see the man's eyes were closed, So I expected he had fainted and hadn't died. I also immediately noticed that the canoe was fully loaded.

Thrown haphazard into the canoe was an array of supplies: camping equipment, ax, setting pole, fishing rods, red boat gas tank and a blue cooler sitting on top of what appeared to be a tattered lifejacket. And the outboard motor was still idling with the shifting lever in the forward position. So whatever had caused the unconsciousness had happened quickly. Underneath the bow seat was an array of empty beer cans, and an empty bottle that bragged it once held a fifth of 90 proof vodka.

I secured the canoe onto shore, walked down the center of the craft, shut off the outboard motor and appraised the unconscious man. In checking his pulse, I found he had a rapid heart beat, was sweating profusely, and his skin was very clammy. By the looks of the mess in the canoe, he'd vomited; He seemed to be having difficulty breathing, a symptom of a diabetic shock induced by low blood-sugar. I took a chance that was the problem and slipped one of my butter rum Life Savers into his mouth. After a minute he regained consciousness. I then gave him sips of orange juice from my afternoon snack. After a few minutes, he began acting confused, stared at me and questioned, "Is that you, Gram?" Then asked, "What are you doing here?" Once he gained his senses somewhat, the man immediately became impatient and irritable.

"Who are you and what are you doing in my canoe?"

"My name is Susan, and I am the wife of Ranger Clark. Are you ok? Can you tell me your name? Do you know where you are?"

"I guess I'm ok and, well you can call me Taunt," the man stammered. "What happened? How did I get here? Why are you standing over me? Hey, who made the mess in my canoe? Did you puke on my floor?" he demanded.

Susan then explained his condition when she found him and that she thought he had experienced a diabetic shock. When asked, the man confirmed he suffered from low blood sugar. Slowly the man's head seemed to clear and he said, "Guess I kinda overdid today. I appreciate your help, just feeling kinda confused." With that he took a half-eaten Three Musketeers candy bar from his right shirt pocket.

"Wait a minute! Did you say you're Clark's wife?"

"Yes, that's right, and I expect Jim to arrive shortly. There is a person missing on the pond and…" about that time in the distance above the alders, a hatch of caddis-flies flew about the green leaves announcing the smooth humming sound of an gas-powered outboard motor. The reverberation grew closer, an indication that the canoe was motoring upstream towards the landing. So Susan stated, "That must be him now."

"I gotta go! I don't mean to be ungrateful, but I gotta go. Supposed to be somewhere else."

"But won't you wait for Jim? He might be able to get

someone to help you drive, or at least load your canoe."

"Nope, gotta go. It's the practical thing to do. I'll be back for my canoe and gear later. And lady, thanks! I think you've saved my life today. I owe ya!"

With that he grabbed a burlap bag from under the bow seat, Strangely the sack, while empty was soaked with blood. Before I could ask, he was in his truck and streaking south up the Blanchette Road towards Second Musquacook Lake and the American Realty Road.

●●●●●●●

That night Taunton had a dream that would haunt the man for the rest of his life. *He is outside standing among a throng of people, watching the crowd. Taunton feels that someone is not just watching, but glaring in his direction. A few feet away, a non-descript man is staring. The individual, not anyone that Taunton recognizes, is someone dressed so he wouldn't stand out in the crowd. Never-the-less, the stranger is focused on Taunton. Appraising the individual for any sign of danger, Taunton sees the stranger is common in appearance, light brown hair, wearing thick glasses behind which are graycold eyes. He is clean-shaven and wearing an off-the-rack suit and tie. Yet it is what was said that causes the perspiration to weep onto Taunton's forehead. Taunton doesn't hear any sound, but agonizes over the words reverberating through his brain.*

"You'll be visiting with me soon." The man seems to say as he threw a smirking glare at Taunton.

"Who are you and what do you want with me?" Taunton mentally questions him.

"You may call me Mr. Beels,[8] and let's just say you'll be going home

---

[8] Author's Note: Mr. Beels, a derivative of Beelzebub. Known as the 'prince of demons,' became a feature of the Salem witch trials. New World Encyclopedia on line. https://www.newworldencyclopedia.org/entry/Beelzebub. Referenced June 9, 2019

momentarily!"

"Home? I have a home."

Not answering, the image gnashed fang-like teeth and faded out of sight.

An experience that Taunton could only describe as a nightmare became fixed in his mind like a frozen puddle of sour cream. He never had the same dream again, although every once in a while he would see Mr. Beels's face in a rear view mirror, or as a reflection in a dirty pool of water. Even so his psyche could not completely erase the vision.

The Ranger's Wife
The Jim Clark Saga
Chapter 18

Burlap Bag

Jim explained the reason why someone would carry a bloody bag…

– Susan's Diary, June 30th, the morning after meeting Mr. Scudder

Arriving at the canoe launch in time to see Taunton's truck leave in a cloud of dust, Jim edged the bow of his canoe onto the pea stone beach, shut off his outboard and asked, "Who was that, and is that his canoe on shore?"

Susan explained the circumstances and the first responder situation she'd found. In response Jim asked, "That truck looks familiar; any chance you caught his name?"

"He just said people called him Taut, why?"

"I suspected that's who it might have been. His full name is Taunton Scudder and a bad apple if there ever was one."

"What do you mean?" his curious wife asked.

"For years Mr. Scudder has roamed these woods

performing one shenanigan after another. The rangers and wardens have been trying to catch him for some time, but he's a sly one. Hmm, wonder why he didn't take his outfit?"

"Well, when I found him he was unconscious, and once he came to he seemed in an awful hurry to get out of here. Any idea why?" Susan asked.

"Expect he's been up to antics on Round Pond. I'll radio the area ranger and tell him Taunton's been around and instruct him to check for any signs of illegal activity such as unauthorized campsites, vandalized buildings, stealing gear, or poaching. Oh, and by the way, the search has been called off. Sorry you drove all the way down here for nothing. But the man has been found."

Gawking at her husband without speaking, Susan queried an explanation, so the Waterway Supervisor continued.

"Two nights ago, the man decided it would be fun to sleep overnight in the crow's nest or observation box on top of the old steel frame of the Round Pond Tower. His plan was to witness and photograph the beauty of an Allagash evening and the following dawn at first light. He explained that that he'd left the canoe upside down on shore, and the wind must have blown the craft into the lake. When he hiked back from the tower yesterday, he got confused and turned north from the hiking trail onto the old abandoned Musquacook Stream tote road. Not recognizing the overgrown deteriorated path, he had to spend a second night in the woods. About an hour ago my ranger saw a man waving from the shore opposite the Turk Island Campsite. He was picked up and returned to the Tower Trail campsite and reunited with his canoe."

Realizing this was the height of black fly season, Susan observed, "That must have been a hard night with all the no-see-ums, gnats and other biting pests."

"Yeah, he was chewed up pretty bad, and sure was glad to see us. I can go home with you, so help me load my gear onto the back of the truck."

Once Jim's canoe was loaded and the couple was headed to Churchill Dam, Susan asked, "Oh, yes, Jim—when Mr. Scudder left his canoe, he carried what appeared to be an empty burlap sack with him, one that looked like it was covered in blood. Would he be apt to have shot a deer or moose and used that to carry venison?"

"Well, I wouldn't put anything past him. But more than likely, he took a pig's head down to the pond; that would account for the blood."

"Why in the world a pig's head to Round Pond?"

"Every once in a while, someone will be naive enough to hire Taunton to guide a fishing trip. Despite all his faults, Scudder isn't any dummy. He knows that when guiding a fishing party, if they catch a lot of fish, then he stands a good chance of getting a very good tip. So a few days before he is scheduled to take someone fishing, Taunton will visit a slaughter house where he'll buy a pig's head. That head will be carried in two sacks in case one bag breaks. Then he'll canoe down to landmarks such as the spring that is just off shore from Back Channel Campsite on Round Pond; there he'll anchor the sack to a heavy stone and sink the first baited bag into the pond.

"He'll keep the outer bag to use another time. Brook trout will smell the blood that seeps out of the bag, along with the bits and pieces of pork and hang around to feed on anything the water current stirs up.

"When Taunton arrives with his sports, he carefully guides them to the spot of the chum where the fishermen will think they have discovered trout heaven."

"Well, that's something! Guess we just never know what people will do."

"Nope, that's for sure. Anyway if you run into Mr. Scudder again, be very careful. Word is that he hates women."

THE RANGER'S WIFE
THE JIM CLARK SAGA
CHAPTER 19

Return to the Woods

While camping near Allagash Lake, we responded to an accident.

— Susan's Diary, early evening, June 30th

When Monday finally came, Margaret arrived at Susan's house and found a 4x4 GMC extended cab pickup parked and loaded. Soon Margaret learned that Susan's youngest son, George, had readied the truck with camping gear, coolers, life preservers, and canoe tied and resting comfortably upside down on the steel rack. Seeing Maggie's arrival, Susan came out of the house wearing a tan shirt, tan trail cargo pants, and L.L. Bean boots, carrying a backpack and two light-colored wide-brimmed exploration style hats. Margaret was pleased to have learned from her earlier trip to Allagash Lake, and so had adorned herself with similar clothing. Now, wondering why Susan was carrying two hats, Susan explained, "If we spend a lot of time on the water we'll need protection from the direct sun."

"But why such a light color?" Margaret asked and continued, "Won't the headgear show the dirt?"

"This is blackfly season and the little pests are attracted to dark colors. Therefore it is best to wear light shades to discourage the biting insects. And we don't really care about getting dirty while frogging around the back country." With that Susan handed one of the hats to Margaret and finished with "I've made our lunch and have cold drinks. I hope you brought a camera, rain gear and bug dope?"

The two woods-women started the borrowed truck and headed off on their adventure. Talking excitedly neither noticed the dusty truck idling nearby. Taunton Scudder had carefully followed Margaret from her apartment, thinking that not being noticed was just fine.

Talking about their experiences, sharing family anecdotes and setting their travel agenda, the time flew by. Before they knew it, they had arrived at the North Maine Woods Caribou checkpoint. Registering to camp at Round Pond near Loon Lodge in T7R14, the party of two planned to tent overnight and the next morning make the hike on the Carry Trail to Allagash Lake, where they would ascend 1800-foot high Allagash Mountain. Once the site of a Maine Forest Service watchman's tower, now all but abandoned, the tall overlook provided an excellent view of the 4,000 acre lake and beyond into the green canopy of the northern forest. The watchman's camp sat at the base of the lake, now occupied by the Allagash ranger who patrolled the lake.

After setting up their tent, the two were about ready to build a campfire when Margaret and Susan heard a loud crash, followed by the screeching of bending metal and broken glass coming from the area of a bridge that crossed nearby Poland Stream. Running to the tent to grab their first aid kid and a sleeping bag, both simultaneously dashed to the pickup, where Susan jumped behind the wheel, started the truck and with spinning tires, backed out of the campsite driveway onto the Ledge Road. By the intensity of the sound, she knew there was no time to waste as the duo quickened to what must surely be a North Woods tragedy.

Arriving at the north side of the Poland Stream Crossing, the responders saw the front of a brown truck hanging diagonally off the end of the planked crossing, threaded so that the vehicle dangled dangerously close to sliding into the brook. The front tire on the driver's side, lodged against a piece of ledge, sat precariously at a 45-degree angle away from the vehicle's fender. The driver's side door was sprung wide open. The front windshield was smashed, with an animal's black head driven partly through the laminated safety glass. The palm of the moose's left antler was inside the truck protruding over the dash with a long prong of the massive velvety rack jutting over the steering wheel only inches from a man sitting unconscious in the driver's seat. The bulk of the bull lay splayed-out over a crumpled hood. With broken legs overhanging to the front grill, the huge body was trapped in place by the penetration of its rack.

Not a pretty picture with open unseeing eyes and a lifeless tongue hanging down over bloodied sharp incisors, the bull's dark colored dewlap or bell dangled listless on the driver's-side windshield wiper. Blood, ruptured from the veins in the soft-covered antlers, had sprayed throughout the interior cab.[9]

The left front tire had received a gash from the sharp rock, and air gurgled from it, sounding much like the final breath of a dying man.

---

[9] Author's note: After the fall mating season, around the beginning of winter, a moose will drop its old antlers and immediately begin growing new ones. In the spring of each year, as moose antlers are growing and preparing for the fall rut, the horns are covered with soft black hairs called velvet. This covering is essentially a skin that supplies nutrients and blood flow to the growing antler bone underneath.

Pulling up to the scene, Susan slammed her truck's transmission into park, shut off the engine, grabbed the emergency responder pack she always kept on the back seat, and without a word to Margaret, rushed to the aid of anyone who might be inside. Unsure what to do Margaret hesitantly followed.

Once at the driver's side door, Susan saw that the vehicle's air bag had exploded into the chest and face of the driver. Opening the buttons on the man's shirt, she found abrasions but no puncture. Black and blue skin framed the scrape. Then Susan recognized the form of a person and remembered that several years before she had found the same man in a similar position. Today the occupant was once again unconscious, laid back against the headrest of his seat with the pointed imprint of the animal's spike cleanly outlined on the man's forehead. The operator's eyes were closed, his mouth open with a trickle of blood seeping from the right corner of his bottom lip. Only this time Susan knew his name—Taunton Scudder.

THE RANGER'S WIFE
THE JIM CLARK SAGA
CHAPTER 20

Sometimes First Responders' First Aid Isn't Quite Enough

Yesterday I finally delivered the ring...
— Susan's Diary, June 31th

Margaret followed Susan's instructions as they unzipped and spread a sleeping bag onto a nearby patch of grass. Working as a team, the two women gently lifted the limp body out of and away from the twisted GMC. While groaning and in obvious pain at being moved, Taunton did not regain consciousness. With adrenalin pumping through every vein in their bodies, the two women didn't even feel the weight of the injured man as they lowered him onto the blanketed ground. Taunton took short shallow breaths and moaned again. *But at least he's breathing,* Susan thought.

Following the steps of triage, Susan checked for extensive bleeding, pulse, and broken bones. When she gently ran her hand down Taunton's chest, he grimaced in pain as cracked ribs shifted in protest. Even when he coughed, he groaned. She

131

determined that he was at Triage Level 2 and needed to be evacuated to a hospital immediately. *But how? They were miles from the nearest ambulance!*

About that time Warden Dennis James pulled into view, quickly appraised the situation and asked Susan how he could help.

Feeling fully relieved, she confidently stated, "He needs to be taken to a hospital. And we ought to hurry before darkness sets in! I've checked him for broken bones, bleeding, and extensive injuries. He should be ok to travel."

"Just so happens," Dennis explained "I've heard radio traffic that indicated that the National Guard MEDEVAC helicopter has returned from a mission to its base in Bangor. I'll contact our dispatch by two-way radio." Without waiting for a reply, Warden James radioed, "2248 to Houlton State Police."

"10-3 (go ahead) 2248," came the immediate reply.

"We have a 10-50 with PI (vehicle accident with personal injury). Please notify MEDEVAC 672."

"10-4, 2248, 10-20 (what is the location) of the scene?

"We are in T7R14 near the intersection of the Johnson Pond Road and the Ledge Road where the bridge crosses Poland Stream. Inform the pilot commander that there is an opening in the forest canopy at the junction of the two roads. There is a very narrow LZ (landing zone) at that split in the road, so the victim may have to be lifted out by the basket. I'll be there with my forest green warden truck with blue lights on."

"10-4, 2248"

Within minutes, the Warden's 2-way radio squawked, "Houlton to 2248."

"10-3 Houlton."

"MEDEVAC 672 advises that the Air Force Command in Virginia has approved their flight plan and the bird is enroute.

They have mapped the location on GPS and their ETA is about 120 minutes."

"Copied Houlton, we'll standby. Also we have a vehicle that needs to be towed to town. Please notify John's Towing Service of Millinocket.

"10-4 2248, also be aware they have been notified that you are the officer on the scene."

"10-4 Houlton, thanks."

"Ok, Susan let's take him over to the large opening in the woodland canopy. That's where we'll meet the helicopter; the bird travels at 120 knots[10] so they won't be long. While we could drive a little closer, I don't want to get too close to the pickup zone because the hovering rotor blades of the air transport are apt to kick up forest debris or dust."

With that the warden backed his truck closer to the injured man and lowered his tailgate. He grabbed the head end of the bag while the two women each took a bottom edge. They gently picked the sleeping bag, using it like a cloth stretcher while keeping Taunton as still as possible, and slid him onto the floor of the truck's bed. Without needing instructions, Susan climbed into the back of the truck, instructing Margaret to move their vehicle as far off the road as possible.

"Houlton to 2248" the radio beckoned.

"10-3 (go ahead) Houlton."

"I have the office of John's Towing Service on the line and they advise John is returning from a call but they will send him to your location as soon as he returns to his base, which should be soon. After he delivers the car he is towing and refuels, his ETA from Millinocket to your location is about three and one-half hours."

"10-4 Houlton, I'll stand by."

---

[10] Author's note: One nautical mile =1.1508 statute mile. Thus 120 knots is about 138 miles per hour.

While waiting, Susan sat in the bed of the truck beside Taunton holding his right hand, monitoring for any signs of cardiac arrest, extensive bleeding, or shock, all the while keeping the mercilessly hungry black flies from eating the patient alive. Margaret helped Dennis take measurements, photographs, and record other important information needed for the official report. Dennis then pulled out a roll of two-inch-wide fluorescent orange flagging tape. Stripping off two six-foot lengths, he and Margaret laid the tape on the ground in X formation. Once stretched and anchored in place by heavy rocks, Dennis explained "This is the marker that identifies the LZ and should be readily visible by the members of the flight crew."

"How many on a helicopter?" the inquisitive reporter couldn't help but ask.

Having worked many search and rescues Dennis replied, "Four. There is the pilot commander, co-pilot, flight medic, and crew chief."

"Why so many?"

"When the bird arrives, it will circle over to observe the scene in a right flight pattern, then drift to the left where all members will appraise the area for any hazard that we may not be able to see. Each one has a specific responsibility and no one will make a move until fully communicated with the others, and a response has been received. Once they are sure the area is safe, the bird will hover between 80-120 feet and began lowering a paramedic and a sked."

Before Margaret could ask about a sked, they heard the warden's radio squeal one more time and a confident voice announced, "MEDEVAC 672 to 2248."

"Go ahead."

"We are five minutes out."

"Roger 672," Dennis confirmed that he understood the nearness of the rescue crew." Margaret and Susan were relieved to hear the whop-whop-whop of the approaching airship."

A few minutes later, another announcement stated, "Two minutes out."

Hearing the sound of a twin-engine National Guard helicopter with its rotation of twirling blades, the folks on the ground watched as the Army green patient medical transport appeared. Further identifying the helicopter as a rescue vehicle were white squares on the nose, belly, and side doors of the UH 60 Black Hawk helicopter. Much to the relief of those on the ground, the white shapes clearly contained very visible red crosses, just as a voice declared, "Ten seconds out."

Hovering high enough for the rotor drift to create motion among the upper branches of the hardwood tree tops, but not low enough to contact tree branches nor stir up road dust, the pilot held the throttle at a constant rpm, and immediately a side cargo opened, and an orange sked was guided to the edge of the bay door. A tag line was fastened to the foot of the flexible plastic roll, and then hooked to a 600-pound hoist, and lowered to the ground.[11]

After the rescue equipment was released, the cable returned to the hovering craft. There, the helmeted medic hooked a nylon-strap harness into a circle ring, connecting herself to a 2-4 point harness. Once buckled securely, the first responder quickly turned her back to the opening, placing her feet on the bottom edge of the open door jamb, she stepped into the air and was lowered to terra firma. On solid ground, the female rescuer unhooked her life-line, which was rewound to the ship, which promptly moved far enough from the incident scene to monitor the situation but not so close that the wash from the

---

[11] Author's Note: A sked is a complete technical rescue litter for confined spaces. Constructed out of plastic, the stretcher becomes semi-rigid when wrapped around a patient. When not in use, it can be rolled into a Cordura backpack for storage. Research found at www.gmesupply.com on July 8, 2012.

rotating blades would affect those conducting the rescue.

Making eye contact with the warden, to recognize his presence, and without a word the paramedic jumped into the back of the warden's truck and went to work. Checking pulse, the rescuer then used a stethoscope to further check Taunton's heart rate, then she checked for broken bones or other obvious signs of distress. Margaret noticed that even with his eyes closed, the expression on the injured man's face was one of extreme pain—*or was it fear?* Maggie couldn't decide which was more apparent.

Dennis backed his truck a few feet closer to the waiting stretcher where the emergency care givers rushed to load Taunton for his ride. The helicopter drifted back into location, and Taunton was carried to the ground and placed on the sked.

While most were looking up, unnoticed by the others, Susan slipped a black onyx bloodstone ring from her hand onto the third finger of the right hand of an unconscious Taunton Scudder.

After completing the medical examination, Taunton was strapped into the rescue apparatus. Once secure, the EMS provider made eye contact with the pilot commander, gave a thumbs-up, and circled over her head clockwise with a right index finger. Margaret caught a quick glimpse of Taunton's face for any sign of extended trauma and detected that his expression seemed to have now changed from a look of absolute terror to one of peaceful calm. As the unconscious Taunton Scudder ascended towards the helicopter, Susan tapped the paramedic on her shoulder and loudly hollered "Can I go too?"

"Are you family?"

"Yes," Susan quickly answered.

Shaking her head, "No, not while the unit is in the air, but if there is a place handy where we can set down, then the lady can go," was said loud enough so all could hear.

"Pulling out his Maine Atlas and Gazetteer, Dennis pointed to a wide spot in the road where the Guy Allen crossed over Ciss Stream. Studying the map, the medic nodded that she understood, and said "we'll land there in about 12 minutes."

The reporter turned towards Susan's truck as the ranger's wife jumped into the passenger shotgun seat. With Margaret driving, Susan gave final instructions, "I am going to help care for Taunton because I want to be there when he wakes up. After you drive me to the landing, please pack up our gear, and drive my truck to meet me at the Millinocket Hospital. I'll show you the way, it's not far."

Within minutes, the map had been studied, Margaret was more confident, and the helicopter had landed on the wide graveled crossing, and Susan had climbed on board and then buckled into a seat belt. For the final time, with all on board and a slam of the heavy side door, the flight headed to the Millinocket Hospital.

Through the Crest of the Red Cardinal

A bulletin about the families of the northern forest

Young girls pulled away from dangerous falls in the nick of time

---

NORTH WOODS GUIDE SAVES THE LIVES OF YOUNG PADDLERS

Master Maine Guide Responds; Identifies crises and Conducts Rescue

Penobscot Valley Times, Bangor, Maine July (PTP)

Two 12-year old girls owe their lives to quick action by an experienced Maine guide. John Wight has canoed the Allagash thousands of times. And if the truth be known, during his 75 trips down the famed river, John has run across almost everything imaginable. But seeing two adolescent females stuck in a canoe at the head of the 40-foot high Allagash Falls, gave the woodsman the scare of

---

his life.

Wight, of Bethel, Maine was camping at Big Allagash Falls when he heard cries for help. Rushing to the head of the falls, John found a turquoise 16-foot canoe with two passengers dangling on the brink of the roaring torrent. The leaders of the group had mistakenly allowed the girls to paddle by the portage trail that led around the falls. When the young paddlers realized their predicament, one jammed her paddle blade through the watery surface wedging the blade between two rocks. When John saw them, the girl in the bow was crying and unable to move. The second girl was holding onto the anchored paddle for dear life.

Reacting quickly, Wight rushed to retrieve his throw rope. Nearby he noticed two men watching so he shouted instructions for them to standby because he needed their help. Over the roar of the falls, John yelled to the girls that he was going to throw them a lifeline. He was able to make them understand not to grab for the rope, but to let the line come to them.

John then made a loop in one end, completing the circle with a bowline knot. Barely able to hear the girls over the rushing roar of the river, he used sign language to communicate to the first frightened girl that once she had grabbed the rope, she should then slip the loop over her head and under both arms.

The guide's first throw swung wide of the canoe. But his second attempt landed on the first girl's lap. While the girl was slipping into the lifeline, John gave his end of the safety line to the nearby men. Once the girl was secure she stepped into the water, and the men pulled the tightened rope so fast, the preteen fairly skimmed across the water.

Once the first female was safe, it was time to retrieve the second. With his hands, John made it clear that she was not to let go of the paddle, but to slip the rope over her head with one hand, while holding onto the paddle with the other. With the line under one arm, the girl was to grab onto the paddle with her other hand and slip the second arm into the loop.

Secured from being carried downstream, the girl stepped into the water once again, and the men pulled the safety line and skipped the frightened girl out of danger, directly into the arms of some very scared councilors.

Without a word, John Wight walked away from the others. He had been so anxious for the young ladies that now the man needed a moment alone.

Well done Mr. Wight, Master Maine Guide. Well done indeed!

Author's Note: This article is based on a rescue accomplished by Master Maine Guide John Wight that occurred on July 10th, 2013. Picture complements of John Wight.

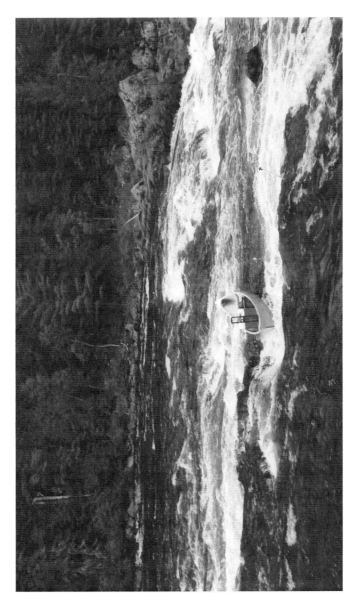

Canoe stuck at the head of Allagash Falls
Courtesy of John Wight

THE RANGER'S WIFE
THE JIM CLARK SAGA
CHAPTER 21

The Chase

Taunton Scudder was livid. He couldn't believe he'd let the girls get out of his sight, but a damn flat tire had slowed him down. He only hoped he could catch the two ahead of him. Yes siree, old Taut had business with the one called Maggie. His left front tire had blown on the Golden Road halfway between Abol Bridge and Rip Dam. Taunton Scudder wasn't happy with the only spare he had, because he realized the 10 ply tire was too worn to use safely. But he was in a hurry with no time to waste. *Yup,* he rationalized, *the practical thing to do was to continue. He could always pull into a sporting camp such as Loon Lodge on the shores of Round Pond and beg them for a tire plug or even to borrow a wheel, if that indeed was where the two ladies are headed.* Taunton figured they might be headed to Allagash Lake because he had learned long ago that the most remote lake was one of the Clarks' favorite haunts.

Once he arrived at the North Maine Woods Caribou checkpoint, he nonchalantly asked Jean, the receptionist, if there had been any traffic through, explaining that he hoped his favorite fishing hole wasn't crowded.

He received the helpful answer that there was a party of

two on the way to camp at Round Pond, planning to hike Allagash Mountain the next day; they had been the only ones through for the last three hours, and "so the fishing spot should be quiet" the polite clerk had been happy to share. Taunton had the answer he needed, now he needed to make time in order to catch up. After registering to camp at Johnson Pond, he jumped into the truck and while putting the hammer down, spun gravel as he headed northwest, but he was soon due to swing north. Hurrying, Taunton didn't even take time to fasten his seatbelt.

Once beyond Hannibal's Crossing, a bridge which spanned the West Branch of the Penobscot River, Taunton swung right onto the Ragmuff Road. Leaving the Golden Road behind, Taunton hit a wide straight stretch of gravel road that ensured he could make fast enough speed to arrive at Round Pond in record time. Passing the turn to Caucomgomoc Landing, Taunton begun to smile; he knew that the Guy Allen Road was just ahead and he'd soon arrive at the Carry Trail that led from the Allen road to Allagash Lake. But when he veered north onto the Ledge Road, nearing the outlet to Poland Pond, his travels took a disastrous twist. That's when the face appeared in his rear view mirror—a common non-descript face, yet one totally focused on Taunton. Piercing eyes, only this time without glasses telepathed a loud and clear message to Scudder's mind that confirmed, "You'll be coming with me soon."

Frightened, Taunton lost his ability to concentrate, and in trying to outrun the vision, he sped up. Suddenly a giant bull moose appeared from the right side of the road and galloped across, passing mere inches from the front grill of Taunton's Dodge. Seeing the animal at the last moment, Taunton jerked his steering wheel to the left, and just as quick, his driver's side tread bare front tire was punctured by a piece of sharp ledge. When the vehicle hit the moose, the hood served as a scoop and picked up the massive bulk sliding it up over and into the windshield. The left palm of the animal's antlers broke through the protective glass with one of its prongs, severely thumping Taunton in the forehead.

As if that wasn't enough, the momentum of the combined weight of the 800-pound moose and the 9,000-pound truck, thrust the conveyance into and caused it to bounce over, an 8"x8" wooden side rail on the bridge. The pickup finally came to rest when the right front wheel trigged against a big stony outcrop that protruded from the rock-strewn bank of the road. This frontal assault caused the vehicle's airbag to explode. The collision and the explosion of the steering wheel's airbag gave Taunton's chest a worse beating than if he was in a boxing ring with two huge fighters pounding on him with massive bare fists.

Taunton, while seriously hurt, wasn't dead, but not far from it. The moose died instantly from a broken neck.

THE RANGER'S WIFE
THE JIM CLARK SAGA
CHAPTER 22

Clean Up

Now that Mr. Scudder was on the way to the hospital, Warden James took pictures and completed the information for the departmental incident report. Once completed, it was time for Dennis to dispose of the moose so the truck could be towed. He hooked one end of a chain around the animal's head, and the other to the trailer hitch of his truck. Slowly he drove the vehicle forward, drawing the large carcass away from its perch and off the truck's hood. Once the antler pulled free of the windshield, the animal's body, already beginning to stiffen from rigor mortis, slid easily onto the ground.

By now, Margaret had returned from dropping Susan off at the landing site, so Dennis invited Margaret to tag along. Moving at a snail's pace, the pickup dragged the remains one-quarter mile down the gravel road to where there was an abandoned twitch road. Once out of sight from traffic, he unhooked the animal from the tow chain and threw the steel links into the bed of the truck. Margaret noted that an unpleasant odor was already emanating from the deceased animal.

Margaret asked, "Shouldn't we process the animal to preserve the meat?"

"Sometimes that works, but more often than not in a collision as bad as this one, the meat is so traumatized and bloody, that it isn't fit for consumption. The coyotes, eagles, ravens and other scavengers will clean it up in no time."

While they waited for the tow truck to arrive, Dennis inquired, "Are you going to stay in the woods tonight?"

"Our tent is all set up at the campsite up the road. I don't really want to be alone, but dark is approaching and I am not sure if I should drive Susan's truck out over these roads at night, with all the moose, deer and other critters that roam after nightfall." The independent reporter didn't say, but she was feeling nervous: this was the first time she had ever been involved in such a traumatic accident. She felt bad for the moose, but it was the helplessly traumatized man that touched her senses. Despite their once poor relationship, she hated seeing anyone or anything hurt.

Nodding his understanding, Dennis offered, "There is a warden camp about 12 miles from here and I always keep a few dry goods and spare clothing there for such an occasion. There are two beds, and once we are finished here, we can pick up the gear from your campsite, and go to camp for the night? Are you able to drive that far?"

"That sounds really good, thank you! And yes, I can make that distance alright." For the second time this year, Margaret had found herself in a position where she didn't want to be alone.

About then she heard the Jake-brake-roar of a diesel powered truck coming too fast, with the operator fighting desperately for control. Rounding the corner, the wide-eyed driver hugged the steering wheel, as the 90,000-pound load swayed from side to side. Dennis jumped and grabbed Margaret, carrying both back beyond the shoulder of the road, and to safety. The eighteen-wheeler kicked up a whirlwind of fine tan-colored dust which rolled in horizontal twister fashion, and choked the two people, then rolled out of sight. Covered with dirt, Margaret laughed when she looked into Dennis's eyes and saw his black eyebrows had been replaced by thick brown grimy lines.

"Guess we'll need a bath as well as a place to sleep. Let's head to camp."

In only a short distance, Margaret turned left and followed the warden's truck to the roadside driveway of a small brown building within sight of Caucomgomoc Lake. Over the entrance door was a black and white sign that proudly announced 'Maine Warden Service.'

Once the entry door opened, Margaret saw a small deer mouse scurry across the floor to get out of sight. After being shut up for some time, the camp smelled musty. Dennis suggested that Margaret should bring her sleeping bag and gear inside while he opened windows to air the cottage, turned on the propane for the stove and lights, and lugged their food coolers onto the porch. Then he said, "I'll go for water," and grabbed two waiting galvanized water pails often used to retrieve fresh drinking water from a nearby spring. "By the way, there are some of my spare shirts, pants, towels and washcloths in that cabinet against the wall by the fridge, if you don't wish to unpack your gear. You can wash up down by the lake to get the dust off. Soap is in the bowl by the sink. I'll clean up when I get back."

While Dennis was gone, Margaret surveyed that night's accommodations and determined that the building was certainly a man's camp. The gray-painted floors could use a touch-up; the windows along each side of the structure could not only use a good cleaning, but bright colored curtains would make the single room homier. *Yes*, Margaret thought, *this dwelling could certainly use a woman's touch.*

There were two single bunk beds, one on each side of the room, with a single four drawer bureau centered under a window between the two cots. There was a woodstove, propane lights, refrigerator and a mishmash of assorted dishes and cups in cupboards that were secured with wooden doors to keep the mice out. A wood box full of dry beech and cedar kindling waited near the camp's Ashley Wood heater. In the center of the room, Margaret saw a small hardwood table and three chairs. The windows had only been open a short time, when a breeze blew in off the lake. The waft replaced the stuffy aroma with a fresh air smell. Only a single year old calendar decorated the walls.

Examining the cabinet by the fridge, Margaret found a red-checked long sleeve shirt, and with towel, washcloth and soap in hand, she headed for the lake. On the shore, she found three well-appointed North Maine Woods campsites. Pleased to see that she had the place to herself, Margaret stepped around a clump of alder bushes, removed her shoes, stockings, blouse, and pants, and stepped into the water. Scrubbing off the layers of dirt and grime, she took a quick dive into the cold water. Then just as she finished washing her hair with the bar soap, and fluffing it dry with the towel, she heard Dennis's truck return. Quickly dressing, when she put on his shirt, it hung down far enough so that she could have worn the top like a nightgown. Robed, she returned to the cabin feeling refreshed and hungry.

Dennis had just finished lugging the pails of water and placing them beside the sink when Margaret walked through the door.

"Glad you found the clean outfit ok, now it's my turn to wash, I'll be right back." Grabbing a clean towel, and a shirt similar to the one Margaret was wearing, the warden headed to the lake. Walking down the road he couldn't help but appreciate how good she looked in his L.L. Bean woodsman's shirt.

Thinking about eating, Margaret suddenly realized that Dennis must be starved as well. Fishing around in Susan's red and white cooler she found all of the fixings for stir-fry. There were frozen shrimp, sweet peas, green beans, broccoli, fresh mushrooms, onions, zucchini, and summer squash. Margaret put water from their cooler into a tea kettle to boil. While she was waiting for the water to heat, she grabbed a cast iron fry pan from the wall and, after washing the camp dust from it, she sautéed the shrimp, and added the rest of the ingredients. While supper was simmering she poured Minute Rice to a boiling pot of water. Looking around she found a half-burnt candle standing in the center of a tin pie plate. Thinking that would be a nice touch she lit the wick and placed the soft illumination in the center of their small table.

Checking the cooler one more time, Margaret also found a loaf of Italian bread, homemade butter, and a bottle of red wine. Adding a quarter cup of wine to the stir-fry, Margaret boldly tipped a small amount into two white ceramic mugs and set the table for dinner.

When Dennis returned from his bath, he was surprised to see only one gas light and the candle lit, but the thing that got his attention was the aroma of dinner. The off-duty warden suddenly realized he was famished.

After finishing the meal, he announced, "Now for dessert." Reaching into a tin canister on the sideboard near the sink, he removed a bag of candy. Foraging until he found two peppermint patties, Dennis gave her one, and together they clicked their mugs in an unspoken salute and drank the last swallows of wine.

Seeing a full moon shining through the cabin window, he suggested "I have a canoe on shore; let's go for a paddle." Once they had donned lifejackets the couple sat comfortably on the craft's cane seats, and with easy strokes, slowly followed the reflected moonlit path on the mirror-calm water towards

Avery Pond. Wispy clouds portrayed a smile across the distant planet, as if the heavenly body was pleased to see the young couple out boating on such a fine night.

Even though it was nighttime, Margaret was amazed with the amount of life around them. In the distance, a family of loons predicted their weather forecast. On shore, a whitetail deer blew an alert at the intruders to his world. Geese honked from a distant cove, and a large bullfrog croaked beside the canoe. Loud yet out of sight, Margaret could hear the sound of dripping water as the antlers of a bull moose broke through the watery surface, as it contentedly chewed on grass plucked from the bottom of the cove. In the moonbeam, a salmon broke through the surface to snatch an insect that the human eye could not see.

Uphill behind the camp a Barred owl called it's 'who-cooks-for-you' in the predator's attempt to encourage the inside mouse to come outside and play. Smiling as he listened to that familiar call Dennis thought, *well, Mr. Owl, perhaps you've just given me the answer to something I been wondering about for some time.*

Heading back to shore, the young reporter, while tired from her earlier involvement with so much devastation, felt calm and ready for a deserved rest.

Finally storing the canoe for the night and arriving on the porch of the woods camp, Margaret reached for the screen door. Dennis lightly touched his companion's upper right arm to gain her attention. When she turned and lifted her chin to meet his gaze, Dennis placed a soft kiss on Margaret lips, a confirmation thank you for a great evening, as one college student might offer to another after having a special date. Without another word, both went inside and silently adjourned to their respective bedrolls.

THE RANGER'S WIFE
THE JIM CLARK SAGA
CHAPTER 23

At The Hospital

Nodding from time to time, Susan sought slumber as she restlessly sat in the hospital lounge chair beside the patient. Not necessarily comfortable, the facility's vinyl-covered furniture served the purpose while she waited for the patient to wake. The woman had been able to catnap, but couldn't capture a sound sleep—not only because of the restrictions of the seat—but also due to the moans and groans uttered by the man lying nearby in the infirmary bed.

He seemed to be having a subconscious dilemma, as if fighting an all-out war. First his head, hot with perspiration, would shake from side to side, as if saying no, then his back would arch and hands and arms would swing wildly away from his body, as if attempting to sweep something aside.

Eventually Susan had moved her chair closer to the bedside, to keep the patient from ripping out his IV's. Then she kept a cool washcloth on hand, so the perspiration could be wiped from his brow. About 4:30 am after she had finished dabbing his brow one more time, and just as the sun was driving away the last of a pitch-black night, he spoke.

"Thank you, Gram. I am so hot and so thirsty, please give me a drink of water." Susan touched the man's parched lips with a straw, and his dry lips hungrily drained the ice water from the plastic tumbler. Opening his eyes, the left one still intensely ringed black and blue from the accident; Taunton Scudder questioned, "You're not my Gram; who are you and where am I?"

"It's ok, Taunton, you're safe. You've had a bad accident, but you are…"

"Hey, aren't you that same woman, Clark's wife, who helped me a while ago by Round Pond? Susan, isn't it?" he said as his mind gathered his wits. Without waiting for an answer Taunton continued. "I was having a dream. I was driving down a dirt road to somewhere, I am not sure where, but in the woods, I think. Can't remember for certain, but I was chasing someone, or something, when suddenly a face appeared in my mirror. It was a dark face that looked more like a snarling beast than human. I stamped down on my trucks throttle trying to out race the image, then everything went black."

"It's ok, Taunton, you're safe. No one is going to harm you now."

"But where's my truck?" Just then Taunton raised his right hand to wipe a small tear from his painful left eye and remembered the damage to his prized possession. That thought was interrupted when he spied the ring on his third finger. Noticing that Susan was closely watching him, nervously he quizzed, "Where did this come from?" Before Susan could explain, he continued, and disclaimed, "I didn't steal it, honestly I didn't steal it! And I…"

"Taunton, please! Wait, I know you're hurt, but let me explain."

For the next hour Susan told him about the accident, the letter she had received from her uncle, and how the ring came to be placed on his finger. She still had three key pieces of information yet to share when Taunton interrupted again.

"It's coming back to me, the crash, there was a face in the rearview mirror. That hideous face was telepathically declaring, 'Come on now, chummy, it is time to pay the piper.' And the image seemed to stay in my mind wherever I looked. I'd turn my head from side to side, but I couldn't shake it from my memory. Then I fell into a totally black void. My gram appeared and said, 'Be patient,' that I was not ready to go with her, there was more to do. It was really weird. Then the hopelessness took control. I've never seen such darkness, not even a hint of a shadow. I could hear a sound, but then I dropped into complete oblivion. Suddenly a bright light exploded in my eyes. I don't know what caused the burst; could it have been caused by the pileup? Oh, I don't know.

"But behind the brightness appeared a different face; it seemed gentle, sending a sensation of kindness, tenderness, hope and peace. Then I felt myself being lifted; I remember thinking *I hope I am not dying*. Does this all sound too weird?" Without waiting for an answer, Taunton continued, "The radiant image of the face spoke to me, I don't know how, but he spoke directly to me. He said 'I have a place waiting for you, not today because you still have work to do on earth. But when the time comes be at ease, my son, you'll be with the father.' But I don't know who my father is. Am I going crazy? It is all so strange!"

Susan reached and took hold of Taunton's hand to calm the man who was so upset and so confused. Taunton continued, "He said, 'but not now.' He instructed that I was to go and help others. He said there were those who needed my support. Please, can you tell me what all this means, please!"

"Yes, I think I can explain. First, you need to know that I am the one who placed the ring on your finger."

"But why?"

"I was asked to do so by my uncle Robert Woodward." And with that Susan read the patient the letter from her Uncle that she had kept for so many years. Before she could tell him the part about the money, Taunton fell asleep.

Two hours later he awoke, and his eyes were much clearer, his forehead less hot. Susan asked, "Do you remember what I read?"

"Yes, you put the ring on my finger and said it is a bloodstone gem, the birthstone of March, the month of my birth. And that the talisman brings good luck, and strengthens the heart. Also I heard you say that the precious stone drives away jealously, evil, and negative energy. But why would anyone want to give me something like that? Must be very valuable; it just isn't practical."

"That's right," Susan said "it is very valuable and you received the gem for a reason. The man who sent it to me, so I could give it to you, was your father. And there is more."

"What? That's not possible. My mother told me my father had died."

"No, he is indeed alive. His name is Robert Woodward and he is a very healthy 77 years old. He did leave you behind that time so long ago, but not because he wanted to. At the time of conception, your dad, my Uncle Robert, was 17 years old and a minor. Underage, his parents had total control and forced the boy to move out of state. That has been troubling him ever since. Several years ago, by searching birth records, he was able to find your name, and wrote me asking that I provide you with this ring and two more items."

In total shock, Taunton lay staring at Susan while he weakly tried to comprehend every word. So she continued. "There is more; in addition to the ring he has put $20,000 dollars in a safety deposit box at the Bangor Savings Bank in Millinocket in your name. After I received his letter, I called Uncle Robert and he said, when you are ready, that he would like you to write and tell him about yourself. And here is the best part. If you want, he is ready to formally adopt you and legally give you his last name." Then she added, "By-the-way, after you speak with your dad, I'd like to have you over to the house for supper to discuss a business proposition. What do you think?" Susan asked, feeling relieved that she had finally been able to do as Uncle Robert wanted.

Not thinking about the ring or the money, Taunton replied, "Taunton Woodward, Taunton Woodward, I kinda like it." Being hit with so much information so quickly, his mind struggled to solve the pieces of an impossible enigma. Even so, his practical mind snatched onto an opportunity for employment, now that he had money in the bank. "Business proposition, you say?"

"Do you remember when I helped you at Henderson Brook Bridge, and afterwards you said 'thanks,' and that you owed me?"

"Yes, I remember you saved my life that day, and now yesterday makes twice that you've come to my aid."

"Well, I'd like you to do me a favor."

"What's that?" a sore and pitiful-looking Taunton Woodward softly replied, now that the magic of the Bloodstone and the pain of the accident had purged his pent-up anger.

Deciding that maybe this was a good time to share the work opportunity Susan said, "I know of a North Woods boys' camp that needs someone to teach city kids how to fish, canoe and hunt. And I think you're the person for the job. Not to mention you'll have a log camp to call home."

"You mean I could get paid to stay in the woods?" Before Susan could answer, another thought hit Taunton like a ton of bricks. "Does this mean that Margaret could be related to me?"

"Yes, Taunton, it does—she's your niece."

THE RANGER'S WIFE
THE JIM CLARK SAGA
CHAPTER 24

The Chest

Margaret now has the contents from the trunk; I hope she finds the material interesting! I wonder what's in it that Jim didn't want me to see.

— Susan's Diary, May 24th

Returning to her apartment, and once parked, Margaret opened the car door to access the rear seat. Sliding the mini-oak strong box towards the open door she was pleased to find that the rectangular box was surprisingly light. The reporter easily carried the container up the stairs to the door of her apartment. Once inside, Margaret placed the coffer near her favorite window, and retrieved the key Jim had left in the letter seemingly eons ago to unlock the strongbox and closely examine the contents in direct sunlight.

The first thing the woman noticed was the glossy finish, a clear indication that this wooden chest was made by a cabinet maker and thus had been a very costly container. Measuring six inches tall, twelve inches wide and sixteen inches long, Margaret found that once she lifted the cover, the interior was trimmed in heart-red velvet. Subconsciously, she remembered that red was often the favorite color for lovers found on Valentine's Day.

The chest wasn't full, but still inside was a mishmash of photographs, miscellaneous papers and other items someone would consider important. But on the very top of the pile was a letter-sized padded envelope. Scribed in Jim's handwriting were the words:

For Maggie only. Please do not open this letter until you have read the manuscript provided below.

Little could she know that inside the packet was a USB flash drive; and if she had been told the envelope contained an electronic memory, she would never have fathomed the data stored on the gig-stick.

Now really curious, and once again assuming her natural role as an investigative reporter, the newswoman set aside the mysterious envelope as requested and shuffled through the contents until she came to several plastic-coiled bound pages. On the front cover in bold script were found the words:

The Ranger's Wife

Flipping to the first page, Margaret found a poem penned by

Jim:

Legends

Sit down dear reader
For there are tales to tell
About hero days
And ne'er-do-wells.

Of canoes, and adventures
Within forest abodes,
Of starlight nights
Hearing loons and toads

Where wind and waves
Challenge many so bold.
Yet present experiences
Still treasured to hold.

Sit down dear reader
For there are tales to tell
Of days gone by
When futures were held.

—James Paul Clark

After reading the verse and skimming the pages inside, Margaret thought that Jim had picked the perfect title for a book. *Is the story something he intended her to write?* Jim's plan was becoming clear.

THE RANGER'S WIFE
THE JIM CLARK SAGA
CHAPTER 25

Final Chapter

I hope that Margaret has everything she needs...
— Susan's Diary, May 25th

Well, this has been quite a ride! Margaret thought. *It seems like yesterday when I first opened the old case and found Jim's letter and the story about Susan. Guess it's time to see what's on the USB flash drive.*

The published author was proud of her first book. The publishing company had approved and made initial payment for her work titled, 'My Maine Man.' And the printing firm had begun a promotion campaign to market the hard-cover novel. Early reviews were so positive that 20,000 copies were now shrink-wrapped with clear plastic, boxed, and readied for shipment.

Seated at her kitchen table, she ran her hand over the first edition proof of the glossy dust jacket cover for the hardcover book. The woman felt pride of accomplishment. From the far corner of her customary seat at the kitchen table, she opened the envelope and grasped the thumb drive that contained information from someone to whom she felt so close:

Foreword
by James P. Clark,
Proud husband and father

To ~~whom it may concern~~ Maggie,

If you're reading this, that means I've gone home. I expected my time would be coming soon, once the doctor told me that there wasn't anything more that could be done about the cancer eating my innards.

But it wouldn't be proper if I left my friends and family behind without giving proper due to my wife Susan; which I have tried to do in the following script.

Reading this document, I beg your patience with any grammar or spelling mistakes found. The lord knows that I never was very good in school. It was just so darn hard to concentrate on my studies when there was so much going on outdoors. As patient a woman as she was, I suspect my English teacher would spin in her grave if she could hear that I've written a book. But Susan deserves it.

In our 40-some years together, the woman has shown the patience of the biblical Job. Always a pretty woman with seemingly delicate features, a body would never know by her quiet demeanor that she has an inner strength not found in many.

Time after time she has put up with the most stressful of conditions, and spent nights worrying about my safety and that of our family. Whether she was settin' the table for a mid-night meal for those exhausted from hours of search and rescue missions, or for soot-covered crews fightin' forest fires, she was always cheerful.

When not feeding visitors, she might conduct first aid, warming hypothermic visitors, or spend days in the bow of my canoe in the best and worst of weather. Her quick smile and determination have seen me and many others through countless dark days.

Here is my humble tribute that I hope you can make into a book about her adventures that some may enjoy. Susan deserves my thanks, respect and deepest love.

Hope I can be around to see how the story comes out.

—Jim

Margaret could only smile when she realized that Jim had been thoughtful enough to include a personalized foreward to perhaps a second book. *Yes*, she thought, *a sequel to* 'My Maine Man' *is definitely in order.*

After reaching the decision to begin the project, Margaret called Susan to give her the news, the draft title, and to ask Susan's blessing with the manuscript. Susan indicated that she wasn't surprised about Jim's request. After all he was always very appreciative of the family atmosphere felt by those who worked so closely together with such a wide range of demands, and, "Yes, please, write the story as my husband had requested."

But Margaret had more inquiries to ask of her friend. "After the accident, we never did get back to Allagash Lake. What was it Jim wanted me to go back to retrieve?"

"Why, my dear he wanted you to return so you'd to get to know Dennis James. Dennis told Jim about the night you and he met at the Cornville cemetery. Dennis also went on to confirm that he would like to see you again, he thought you had the deepest hazel green eyes he'd ever seen.

"After listening to his friend, Jim decided that you two were the perfect match, but he didn't want to say so because you might think he was meddling. So Jim, without telling you, had asked the warden to meet you at the Ice Cave Campsite where he could teach you to fly fish. That's why the packet of trout flies were in the cask for you. He wanted the two of you to have an opportunity to better get to know one another."

Feeling slightly embarrassed about the suggestion of a relationship, the reporter changed the subject. "So the mushroom in the wooden urn must have been a Chaga?" Margaret suddenly realized.

"That's right. The growth was my husband's way of letting you know the treatment he was using to get better."

"One last question?"

"What's that, Margaret?"

"At the church remembrance near the podium, there was the prettiest painting of a white pine with a red cardinal sitting on the tree's limb. What does the landscape represent?"

Smiling Susan replied, "Why, that's a likeness of our future stone at the cemetery, Jim felt that it was the perfect symbol of our years together and a proper display of a couple's love. The tree represents Jim's strength and longevity, and the female red cardinal on the limb, that's a representation of my devotion to family. Jokingly, Jim always said that he preferred it to be considered a symbol of me being held in his arms."

That evening Margaret had a surprise caller. Answering the

knock on her apartment door, there was a grinning Dennis James dressed to impress, standing straight and proud, holding a bouquet of wild flowers. Margaret could smell a light fragrance of musky cologne. Immediately the image of his hug and earlier kiss flashed through her mind. Pleasantly surprised to see him, she exhibited a huge grin, and then heard Dennis invite, "Margaret, do you have time to go to dinner? I have a favor to ask."

Thrilled to see the handsome woodsman, the lady nodded in the affirmative and answered, "I'd love to and please call me Maggie. Jim would like that."

THE RANGER'S WIFE
THE JIM CLARK SAGA
EPILOGUE

A senior citizen shifts the transmission of his 4x4 into reverse and backs up an abandoned logging road. His right-footed leather hiking boot lightly throttles the accelerator of the buckskin brown truck gently over a slope-ledged, rock hard surface of what was once a very busy right-of-way. The road, forsaken years before, snakes between partly-vegetation-filled ditches, and the truck quickly becomes concealed by the growth of larch and alders. The secondary succession of vegetation provides the perfect blind to hide the old ranger's transportation. Out of sight from anyone who might pass, the man parks the vehicle at a spot approved by a landowner friend years before; a convenient storage spot that the old woodsman has used often since his retirement.

Exiting the cab he stores the ignition keys inside the door of the fuel cap. Once his dunnage is unloaded, he shifts a camouflage backpack onto his shoulders. With a huge right hand our voyager grabs an 1894 Marlin 38-40 rifle and strides along a nearly invisible path, the trail once served as the route to maintain a galvanized telephone line, a deep woods communication link that connected occupants of the northern forest to the outside world. It ended (or began, depending on which way you headed) at the oak hand-crank wall phone secured to the wall of the Maine Forest Service camp on Allagash Lake.

Thinking about the wire exchange used years before two-way radios and satellite receivers, today's gent pauses for a second when he discovers a beehive-shaped teal-colored glass insulator still wired to a leaning cedar. Forgotten, the three-inch by four-and-a-half-inch conductor once had been wired ten feet off the ground to prevent the silver-colored conduit from touching soil and grounding out, terminating the ability to make a phone call.

Further along the duff-covered trail, our friend passes a corroded metal sign nailed to a spruce. Rusted and faded the marker confirms he is walking on the old *Trail to Allagash Mountain Lookout Tower.* The letters are still visible only because years before, a steady hand had used a small artist's brush and white paint to preserve the words, a second clue that this once had been a well-traveled route. Midway through the forest transitional zone, the man passes by aged white birch hardwoods, and smiles when he notices a good supply of Chaga mushrooms. Walking over a small plank, the only reminder of a logged crossing, he looks down at Little Johnson Stream. In the shade of the wooden walkway he sees a brook trout with its fins gently moving back and forth, as the fish waits for a caddis nymph to float by.

After three-quarters of a mile, he arrived at a canoe stored upside-down on the bank of a small stream. Turning the canoe over, he's pleased to find the stowed paddle and lifejacket still in place. Here he places his pack into the bow and pushes out into the easy flow. Jim smiles, nods, and thinks *it's good to be home.* Another half mile downstream, the paddler eddies the craft so the bow points upstream, lands on shore, coming to rest on a rock outcrop, confident that anyone paddling downstream would pass by this landing with nary a notion a canoe was deposited nearby.

Another 60 yards into the forest, he arrives at a small cabin sitting in a sunlit glen. A solid structure built years before is just big enough to allow a man, a woman, a golden retriever and perhaps a child, overnight accommodations. Sitting on a knoll under towering white pine, the location ensures that the inhabitants won't be easily noticed from the river. It will allow a breeze from the lake to keep blackflies at bay, while still providing a brief view of blue water. A path from the northeast side of the residence leads 70-feet to a hardwood clearing, where a cedar plank seat encourages any observer with the opportunity to scan a large portion of the 4,000 acre lake, unseen.

Surveying the area outside camp, he sees that all is well and the dwelling hasn't received any apparent unwelcomed guests. The deer have nearly cleaned off the salt lick he maintains for his friends, and two Grey Jays tweet their birdie 'hello' to their human neighbor. A red squirrel harvesting seeds from a pine cone can't be bothered long enough to stop eating to scold a chattered greeting. A red-headed pileated woodpecker drums for bugs on a distant hemlock.

He opens the door, an entry never locked because the structure had been built so well-concealed that the owner doesn't need to worry about unexpected human visitors. Accustomed to inventorying his surroundings, he finds that the tidy one-room dwelling is in order. He is relieved to see that he left the white-birch-covered wood box full of dry beech, a firewood with high BTU's which, when burned, emits a nearly invisible smoke through the cabin's chimney. Even when wood is used in the cabin's Star Kineo cook stove with a hot apple pie in the oven, the stove burns clean. The man notices that time has not diminished the yellow and green colors of an Indian chieftain in full-feathered headdress, a likeness painted years before. The design, originally etched on a wood box covered in white birch bark, was created by a famous woman who once taught school at

Churchill Dam. [12]

Helen Hamlin's wood box
From the T. Caverly Collection

---

[12] Author's Note: This photograph of the wood box painted and used by Curly and Helen Hamlin when the couple lived in the game warden camp on Umsaskis Lake in 1938-39. Her description of creating the wood box may be found on page 70 of the book 'Nine Mile Bridge' written by Mrs. Hamlin and copyrighted in 1945. Mrs. Hamlin taught school at Churchill Dam for one year beginning in 1937, and eventually turned to painting portraits to help her family's financial situation.

Gazing at the location of the sun he guesses there is time to do a little evening fishing and scans the lake to see if his wife is on the way. Moving with an ease that comes from working years in the Maine woods, the man thinks, *Yup this is where I belong. Not sure how long I'll remain, but with the help of the Chaga, and when Susan and Sandi are here, I'll be just fine.* Smiling, the man speculates, *who knows? my Great Aunt Emma lived to be 109; that certainly seems like a reasonable goal.* But before fishing, first he readies a tea pot for an end-of-the-day cup of the dark colored mushroom drink.

On the south end of Allagash Lake, a senior lady and golden retriever walk the mile-long Carry Trail to a canoe hidden 100 yards east of the Carry Trail campsite. By forenoon Mr. and Mrs. Dennis James had dropped off the elderly lady, with a pack basket full of fresh supplies, at the barrier that prevents vehicle access to this most wild part of the Maine woods. Hiking over the rough and rocky trail, the lady is thankful for the gift of a hiking staff especially created for her by the craftsman Mr. Tasker, owner of *Dick's Sticks* of Plymouth, Maine.

Loading her backpack into the front of the canoe, she pushes the slim water vehicle halfway into the inland sea. Sandi immediately assumes her accustomed place in front of the middle thwart and stares up the lake, looking for her master. Overhead from the bottom limb of a white pine, Mr. and Mrs. Red Cardinal trill the lady a welcome home.

Rising early that morning to get an early start in order to make camp before dark, she had stuffed the unopened previous day's packet of mail into a waterproof bag. Knowing that her husband would enjoy being the one to open any correspondence, she hadn't thumbed through the six or so envelopes. If she had, then Susan would have found a registered letter from the Brewer Family Cancer Institute addressed to Mr. James Paul Clark in Millinocket. Above the addressee bold letters ordered:

This Document only to be opened by Addressee or his Power of Attorney.

Accepted and signed for by their daughter, the important-looking post had been covered by other pieces of mail.

In a scene reminiscent of an earlier time, when Native Americans traveled across water by birch bark, the lady is pleased to see the lake is a flat calm. From past experience she knows she should be at camp well before dark, where her husband surely will have a pot of brewed tea waiting. She thinks, *it's good to be home; maybe there will be a chance to do a little fishing tonight.*

Around this same time Warden and Mrs. James are driving their state-issued four-wheel-drive truck to Caucomgomoc Lake where they will meet a waiting pontooned aircraft which will lift the couple with their months-worth of supplies to their new remote log home. Only married a short time, and with no need to make eye contact, the couple simultaneously slide their arms across the seat until their hands meet. Lost in thought, each smiles with news of their own, not only pleased with the prediction, but also the realization that, at least for a while, they'll have some darn nice neighbors.

•••••••

In a Cornville cemetery, at the farthest back part of the grave yard, a resilient stone sits and waits. The 28-inch-by-18-inch black marker, much different than traditional gray headstones, seems out of place, but the memorial depicts a significant image. The polished face of the dark granite marker is color engraved with two images. The first figure is an illustration of the majestic eastern white pine; sitting predominately on the farthest part of the lowest limb of the tree is a lone songbird—a slightly colored red cardinal.

First-time visitors may wonder, and yet not completely understand, that the tree represents the strength, spirit and individuality of Maine, such as found in a husband. Historically the evergreens, 24 or more inches in diameter, were called the King's Pine. In the 17th and 18th centuries, standing trees were marked with broad arrows to indicate they were reserved to be used as ships' masts for the King of England's navy. In Colonial times these softwood giants would have diameters of more than 36 inches. But in the 21st-century, the tree is treasured for its lumber and durability. It i a softwood so well respected that the tree's seed, the pine cone and tassel, serve as the Maine State flower.

The colorful songbird waiting on the limb of the old-growth Pine is a scene that depicts the longevity of true love —symbolic of a steadfast relationship—as found in a devoted wife. Perhaps best described in the poem by Hazel Gaymor:

"To love in the heart of those we love —is never to die."

At its base, the only characters chiseled in stone are:

James Paul Clark	Susan Ann Clark
Born November 16, 1954	Born February 8, 1956.
Left this earth_____	Left this earth____

POSTSCRIPT

As for our friend Taunton Woodward, after eating an evening meal, throughout which ensued a pleasant conversation of stories about flora, fauna, old-time logging history, and characters each had met, Susan suggested they adjourn to the den for coffee. Rising from the dining table, a partially-healed man sorely follows the hostess into the well-apportioned living area and to other surprises. Seated, and after coffee was poured, Susan said, "Don't take this wrong, Taunton, but you have quite a reputation."

"But," Taunton said as he tried to interrupt.

"Please, let me finish. As I said, you've been known for many years in a bad light as being quite a character. However, I think you are a better person than the one portrayed. I can't possibly know all that you've been through, and I don't need to know. However, I have seen you almost die twice." Moving to sit beside Taunton on the couch to emphasize her caring, Susan continued, "My husband Jim belongs to a fraternal organization which I think would be a good support structure for you."

"What's that?"

"You ever hear of the Masons?"

"Aren't they a secret organization?"

"I prefer to say that they are a brotherly support group that, through their fellowship, helps others; such as yourself, Taunton, to be better people. You told me many years ago that you owed me. Now, I would like to collect on that debt."

"How's that?" Taunton asked with sparked curiosity.

"In Millinocket there is the Nollesemic Lodge #205 in Masonic District 24, a part of the Grand Lodge of Maine. My husband picked up a membership form and we are inviting you to submit an application.

"But I've never joined anything in my life!"

"Perhaps that is part of the trouble—will you apply? I do not know any of the requirements, but Jim has said that it is up to the committee of brothers whether you are accepted or not. Here is an opportunity for you to be a part of an age-old positive support structure."

Taking the form, the quiet man skimmed it over, and confirmed, "I do owe you a lot, and by the way, you actually remind me of my Gram; until recently the only woman who really cared. Yes, I'll submit the request to join."

"Perfect, I thank you, and I am sure you won't regret it. I now have one final request."

Bending over, Susan picked up a page-worn book from the coffee table and handed a King James Bible to her dinner guest and now friend saying, "This is for you."

Without a word, Taunton took the book and opened to the first page where he read the following inscription:

This book given to Robert Woodward on graduating from high school. We trust it will bring you peace.

•••••••

Today a fully healed and content Taunton teaches outdoor skills at a children's camp; spending his days in the woods and waters of Maine where he once again falls asleep most nights listening to the comforting calls of the loons and an occasional whip-poor-will. The second and fourth Thursday of every month you can find him at the Nollesemic Lodge #205 as a

Master Mason.

Mr. and Mrs. Dennis James have retreated to a cabin in the deep woods where the warden was assigned to protect our animal friends; where, over time, he rescued many sportsmen and women from dilemmas encountered as they ventured into the most remote part of Maine's northern forest.

Published author and very pregnant Maggie James, continues writing, while she watches for job postings that announce work opportunities on the Allagash Wilderness Waterway. After all, raising a new son on a nationally designated wild and scenic river is the practical thing to do. She now even knows someone who would help teach the young lad how to handle a canoe and the proper way to cast a fly rod.

As for Mr. and Mrs. James Paul Clark, they are living comfortably in a small cabin off the grid. People on a pilgrimage to Allagash Lake often recount that at first daylight, or sometimes at twilight, they have seen a couple fishing from a green canvas canoe while a golden retriever contently sits and watches. "Oddly the couple," as campers have reported, "never seems to carry any overnight gear or occupy a campsite."

The End

Tim & Susan Caverly

My Diary

(Use these pages to begin a diary of your own.)

The Ranger's Wife

(more of My Diary)

Tim & Susan Caverly

(more of My Diary)

The Ranger's Wife

(more of My Diary)

Tim & Susan Caverly

(more of My Diary)

GOLDEN RETRIEVER AWARD OF EXCELLENCE

Sandi and Deborah Sue Glenn discussing the benefits of the herbal pain remedy
PRIM; available at Maine's
www.sunshine apothecary.com

Sandi, the golden retriever says, "I recommend *The Ranger's Wife*
for an intriguing, yet still pain-free read.

ABOUT TIM AND SUSAN CAVERLY

Tim and Susan having a date night
Photograph from the T. Caverly Collection

Tim Caverly is a Maine author who has written and published ten books about Maine. He is a member of the Nollesemic Lodge # 205 of Masons, 'Son of the American Legion' Post 80 in Millinocket, and an honorary member of the Board of Directors for Houlton's Starbright Children's Theatre. Tim is a graduate of the University of Maine at Machias—the eastern most university in the U.S.

In 1999 Tim retired from his position as Regional (Park) Supervisor of the Allagash Wilderness Waterway for Maine's Department of Conservation. After retirement he worked several years as the Maine Director of Public Employees for Environmental Responsibility.

Several of Tim's short stories have been printed in newspapers, magazines and outdoor journals. He has also presented creative writing lectures at Young Authors Camps, as well as many Maine youth summer camps. Tim's second book "An Allagash Haunting" was adapted into a stage play and has been performed numerous times. The story was also transcribed into a radio classic program.

By early 2019, through their "New England Reads" literacy project, Tim, Susan and Frank Manzo Jr. had provided 252 PowerPoint programs to over 8,600 students from Maine to Vermont. In addition, to encourage literacy and learning about New England's natural world, they have donated over 1,800 Allagash Tails books to 175 New England schools.

After accompanying his fire warden dad, beoing on patrol with Baxter Park Ranger brother Buzz and his 32 years as a Maine Park Ranger, Tim has lived in all four corners of Maine. Readers can be confident that his stories are based on personal experiences and knowledge of our State's history and landscapes.

Along with Tim, **Susan King Caverly** is a resident of Millinocket. As a young child she often stayed with her grandparents Harold and Elsie Kidney in their camp in the Maine woods, as they worked for Great Northern Paper Company. Harold was a river-driver foreman on the West Branch of the Penobscot River, and Elsie aws the first female cook at the GNP Boom House on Ambajejus Lake, a building that is now listed on the Register of National Historic Sites. As a young girl, Susan often went on river duty with her grandfather, where she served as bow-weight in the paper company's work boat. When not on the water, the little girl would sit with lumberjacks at the dinner table, jabbering contently during a time when North Woods protocol required rivermen to remain silent while eating. After their meal, Susan would sit on the porch where the woodsman would help her practice rope knots in order to earn Girl Scout merit badges.

Growing up she spent a great deal of time with her parents, Homer and Joan King, camping and hiking in Baxter State Park She eventually became a Councilor-in-Training at the Girl Scout camp Natarswi, located on the shores of Togue Pond.

During her Stearns High School years, Susan was inducted

into the prestigious National Honor Society. After graduation she attended the University of Maine at Machias, where she earned a B.S. Degree in Business with a concentration in Education. During college, Susan worked summers as an information clerk in Baxter State Park.

After their marriage, Susan went to work for the Department of Conservation Bureau of Parks and Lands. She served as a Park Receptionist and Regional Secretary for 20 years, and 5 years as Regional Secretary for Public Lands, often serving as public relations (and sometimes political) buffer when Tim or park rangers weren't available.

Susan felt that the real chore of a ranger's wife was learning to understand. For example, when her husband was overdue coming home; missed a meal or showed up late to a birthday party, it didn't mean that her partner was in harm's way. So the woods-woman chose to believe that all was well unless she heard otherwise.

Following retirement, Susan worked nine years in the Millinocket School System where she assisted students with special needs.

Today Tim and Susan live in Millinocket, Maine where they, when not writing or public speaking, raise golden retrievers. Tim and Susan have one daughter who enjoys outings with her own family and learning about New England's natural world.

Susan helps Tim write books, and the couple travels throughout New England speaking at libraries, sporting organizations, retirement communities, and schools to share their personal experiences of life in the Maine woods.

ABOUT FRANKLIN MANZO JR.

Frank shares his love of art with his daughter Bella.
Photo by Gabriel Manzo

Frank was born and raised in Millinocket, Maine where he attended Stearns High School. After working as a software engineer for over 25 years, he returned to his family homestead in Millinocket. Frank is a noted artist, and his photographs and illustrations are popular and enjoyed by all. Frank's prior work experiences include: editor of a local newspaper, teaching in the Millinocket School System, and he is currently a Database Specialist at Eastern Maine Medical Centers in the centers Performance Improvement/Data Management Department. Frank has always enjoyed pursuing art and sharing his drawings with his children. He is an avid hiker, camper, and outdoorsman, and enjoys being able to share his love of the North Maine Woods by illustrating for Allagash Tails.

ALLAGASH
TAILS

Ask for all books in the Allagash Tails Collection
at your local bookstore.

Volume 1: **Allagash Tails – Marvin & Charlie** (Illustrated Children's Book)

A 'tall tail' for the ages!

A collection of 'tall tails' for the whole family. Perfect to be read around the campfire or when tucking the little campers into bed. Swim with Marvin Merganser, a fish-eating duck that usually has very bad luck, but his sympathy for a watery neighbor changes all of that. Feel compassion for Charlie, the White Water Beaver. Charlie is cross-eyed and narrow tailed and dreams of a better life. See if he can overcome life's adversities in this charming "tail" for the ages.

Volume 2: **An Allagash Haunting—The Story of Emile Camile** (Book One of Olivia's Journey)

"A damping cloak of darkness approaches…"

Olivia's mother had always said that a trip on Maine's Allagash River was not like any other canoe trip. But she would never explain what she meant. A violent thunderstorm is building as ten-year old Olivia is canoeing and camping deep in the Maine woods with her family. Travel with her as she uncovers the mystery and learns about one of our nation's wild rivers, where she discovers an unknown secret about her mother when she comes face to face with the last thing anyone could ever imagine.

You can also produce the play version of this wonderful tale of a haunting in the Allagash. The script was adapted from Tim's book by Barbara Howe Hogan of the Houlton Bright Star Children's Theatre, of Houlton, Maine, and is available for live performance in schools, amateurs, and professionals.

Contact www.leicesterbaytheatricals.com for further information.

Volume 3: **Wilderness Wildlife: Animal Antics** — (Illustrated Children's Book)

Who was Henry David Thoreau anyway?

Ever since Henry David Thoreau visited the Allagash, thousands of people have flocked to Maine's North Woods to enjoy deer, moose and the call of the loon. But do we really know what goes on in the animal world? What if we could talk to the animals,—what might they say? Find out by reading "Wilderness Wildlife."

Float with Carl the Wise Old Canoe as he travels the Allagash and learns of the animal antics that his Allagash friends are having. Delight with Oscar 'the awkward Osprey' when he falls out of the sky and finds the most unusual thing ever. Be astounded by the chilling 'tale' about how two young hunters tumble into trouble during The Attack at Partridge Junction. In this edition of Allagash Tails enjoy the playful behavior of Oscar the Osprey as he learns to bellywaump. Float with Carl, the guide's twenty-foot canoe, as he discovers the new and unbelievable antics of his Allagash neighbors.

Volume 4: **A Wilderness Ranger's Journal – Rendezvous at Devil's Elbow**

(Book Two of Olivia's Journey)

In the dark of night there is always something else!

There is always a special feeling to the Allagash (those of you who've been there know); a sense of adventure, the thrill of getting away from it all!

In the sequel to the popular *An Allagash Haunting*, the three family members have only been on the water for four days and already Livy has experienced enough to last a lifetime.

In this mystery-adventure, paddle with Olivia and her family as they canoe Northern Maine's most famous wilderness river The Allagash. Looking at a map of their travel route they find there is a bend in the river called "The Devil's Elbow" in front of them. They wonder what they could possibly encounter next as the current carries them down stream against their will. In the darkest of the night, a shadow lingers, hiding beyond the reach of the lantern's fingers of light. It remains obscure in the midst of the evergreens and old growth. Among the campfires and s'mores, a bone-chilling draft embraces all. Shivering, they draw our coats tighter to protect against the rawness.

Volume 5: **Headin' North: A Tale of Two Diaries** (Book Three of Olivia's Journey)

Red sky at night,

Sailors delight.

Red sky at morning,

Sailors take warning...

Remembering her grandfather's dire weather forecast, a young girl stares at the morning's inflamed sky. Traveling by canoe deep in the Maine woods is not where Olivia should be, but that's exactly where she is. Suddenly lightning strikes the nearby shore, causing the girl to nearly jump out of her skin. Looking towards the sound, the youth sees the apparition of a log cabin floating over a vacant lot. Inside the building a young ranger is looking out; the pair exchange unintended smiles, under the aroma of a blown-out match, the scene fades. This is the third and final book of the exciting North Maine Woods trilogy, detailing a family's paddle down a famous American river. During the day the girl records her unbelievably wild adventures, and each night she listens spellbound while her mother reads incredible tales from the grandfather's hand-written journal. Olivia and her family have 53 miles left to complete their Wilderness Allagash canoe adventure. Then, in the middle of a remote lake, they see storm clouds gathering. Thunderheads build and lightning strikes. Bolts of forked electricity char the ground of the nearby shore; causing the electric charge to open a portal through time. This cosmic doorway allows a granddaughter and her grandfather, separated by the years, to write in their diaries at the same celestial instant. In "Headin' North" the reader will discover stories from today and yesterday.

Volume 6: **Solace • Allagash Lake Reloaded** (Book One of the Ranger James Clark Saga)

If your grandfather could give you anything—what would it be?

During his third year of college, a young man is forced to abandon school and leave his classmate and friend Susan behind. Jim returns to the family farm only to face one hardship after another.

Broke and with debt mounting, Jim's world falls apart. Then one day, while cleaning out the attic of his now-empty colonial home, Jim discovers an envelope, yellowed with age.

The letter is from a grandfather he's never met, and it instructs Jim to go to Allagash Lake and retrieve an heirloom "for the sake of the family!" Follow along as Jim treks deep into the Maine wilderness to recover a grandfather's keepsake, and stumbles onto a mystical path to the past.

In this mystery-adventure, canoe with Jim Clark as he searches for the bequest and encounters a mystical energy highway where he learns more than he really cares to about the future.

Volume 7: **The Ranger and the Reporter** (Book Two of the Ranger James Clark Saga)

What's in a name? "A rose by any other name would smell as sweet. But a Trillium is still a stinkin' Benjamin." -- *Jim Clark*

Cub reporter Margaret Woodward has been given an assignment she doesn't want! The editor for the Penobscot Basin Times has sent her to interview retired ranger James Clark, a secretive Maine woodsman. Others have tried to write the man's story, but no one has been able to break through the outdoorsman's blunt exterior. Instructed to *complete the report,* Margaret visits Bangor's assisted living community; where "old man Clark is expected to live out his final days."

In this sequel to the popular book *Solace,* tag along with our reluctant newspaper trainee who struggles to uncover the mysterious ordeals of a wilderness ranger. Will she 'get her story' or will Margaret discover there is more to a person's life than waiting for an inscription on a tombstone—even hers?

Volume 8: **Andy's Surprise** (Illustrated Children's Book)

Andy -- What A Moose! Sometimes surprises can go two ways!

The story is about a Maine moose who one day receives the biggest surprise ever. Geared for the three-year old and up, the tale takes place in the heart of New England's wild river, the Allagash. The account is based on an event I witnessed one day while working as a Maine park ranger. The publication, an illustrated 600-word book, contains 16 full color drawings and 4 coloring pages. 'Andy's Surprise' is perfect for the young of age and young of heart. All readers, in Maine or out of Maine, will enjoy this treasure from the wildest part of the northern woods.

Volume 9: 'Tis the Season In Maine

**"Mom, will you make Daddy go to bed?" the little girl cried.
"Santa will never come if he doesn't come upstairs!"**

Imagine if you will, a literary journey that allows you to travel back to

Christmas Day in 1953. Become a member of a family whose roots are traced back to the Mayflower, and share in their traditions of Christmas holidays and experiences through the 20th and into the 21st century.

In this book of four short stories, travel from the villages of Cornville to Corinth, from Machias to Millinocket and then venture north into the heart of the Allagash Wilderness. Read about a typical New England family's hopes, customs, and sometimes… their fears.

But we must wonder, will the Spirit of Christmas always make it through economic hardships, absence of family members, and storms that leave snowbound whole communities? What is it that makes Christmas so special, the gifts, the people, the food, the religious celebrations, or could it be all of those and even something more?

Volume 10: **The Rangers Wife** by Tim and Susan Caverly (Book Three of the Ranger James Clark Saga)

"Behind every successful man is an amazing woman, and thank goodness Susan was there!" — Ranger James Paul Clark

Susan, the wife of ranger Jim Clark has spent her whole life in the Maine woods, but Mrs. Clark never realized just how resourceful she could be until her husband went to work on the Allagash Wilderness Waterway. Tag along with our lady-of-the woods as she learns early-on in life about deadheads only to discover that there are many dangerous things in the Maine woods and every one of them could instantly make her a widow.

Volume 11 — Coming in 2022

Visit us at

www.allagashtails.com

Also visit us at

www.leicesterbaybooks.com

MORE FROM ALLAGASH TAILS

Outreach Programs

Invite the creators of Allagash Tails to visit your school, library, or organization, to hear firsthand the 'story behind the story.' In an hour-long multi-media, PowerPoint program; author Tim Caverly will present tales about Maine and the North Woods as you've never heard before. Learn about the natural and logging history of this nationally protected watershed.

Play adaptation of *An Allagash Haunting*

Watch the characters Olivia, Jacquelyn, Kevin, and Allie the golden retriever come to life in the stage creation of the story about family, friends, and Maine's North Woods legacy. Contact us at www.allagashtails.com for information on how to bring this production to your community.

"An Allagash Haunting -- a radio classic"

Hear the story as told on Houlton radio station WHOU 100.1 FM in the fall of 2012, while over 120 scenic, historic, and wildlife pictures flow across the screen. Listen to the call of the loon, hear the quickness of old-time French-Canadian music. Thrill with the cast of characters as a family travels to the Maine woods, as only a PowerPoint program can describe. Available on CD.

Coming Soon:

Watch for more about Maine's premier natural areas and other stories that are "classic" Maine.

For more information about our books and programs
see www.allagashtails.com

like us on

Partners in the stories of the
Allagash Wilderness Waterway

Made in United States
North Haven, CT
23 February 2023

33062683R00119